# SIGNS OF LOVE

### Love Signs - Book One

## HANNAH KANE

Published by Blushing Books
An Imprint of
ABCD Graphics and Design, Inc.
A Virginia Corporation
977 Seminole Trail #233
Charlottesville, VA 22901

Hannah Kane
Signs of Love

Print ISBN: 978-1-64563-551-2
v1

# Chapter 1

I f someone would have told her six weeks ago that she would be standing with her nose pressed in a corner, jeans and panties around her ankles, waiting for what she knew was going to be an epic spanking—she would not have believed any of it. She had considered herself an independent woman, didn't even have a boyfriend, and even if she did, he was not going to be the boss of her! But here she was —waiting. Lydia didn't know how long she had been there but it seemed like an hour.

In truth, she knew this spanking was coming, but there had been so much drama in the last few days, she had been ignoring its inevitability. Ever since Lydia had completely ignored Cade's warning and put herself in real danger, she knew she would end up over his knee.

It had been a close call. Lydia had been frightened out of her wits as had Cade. But Cade had also been furious that she put herself in that position. Due to circumstances, he could not, nor did he want to, spank her immediately. It took twenty-four hours for the situation to calm enough to address her punishment.

For a while, Lydia thought she might escape a spanking. Cade had been frightened for her safety and declared his love for her in a touching speech. But then he announced his intention to make sure she never did anything so reckless again, and she would be paying the price.

He had sent her to put her nose in the corner of the bedroom, to wait with her bottom bare. She was to be thinking about the reason for this spanking. And she was. The way she was forced to stand caused her bottom to stick out as if just asking to be punished. As she felt the cool air of the bedroom caress her backside, she thought about how it would soon be set on fire by Cade's paddle-like hands. It was going to be so painful! And the fact that if she had followed his directions, none of this would have happened, made her feel even worse. Tears were already silently coursing down her cheeks.

Finally, she heard him come into the bedroom. He stopped and she knew he was looking at her. Cade was struck with her beauty every time he saw her and now the sight of her with her bare bottom waiting for him expectantly and sporting a large red handprint that he had applied as he sent her to the bedroom, almost gave him second thoughts. But then he remembered the situation she had put herself in and could have avoided if she had listened to him. He never wanted to be that frightened again. He wanted this spanking to be one she would remember so that she was always more careful.

Lydia wanted to beg forgiveness and make promises—anything to avoid what she knew was coming. But Lydia knew that when Cade had decided to spank her, there was no going back. So, she waited quietly as he sat on the corner of the bed and called her over.

"Come here, Lydia," he said in that deep, rumbly voice she would find so sexy at any other time.

She turned around and looked at him then. He crooked his finger at her and she hobbled the short distance to where he sat. He placed her in between his muscular legs, held her wrists and looked into her eyes.

"You know why you are here so we are not going to talk about it. However, I am not sure you understand how disappointed I am that you went behind my back and did something you knew was dangerous. I don't want it ever to happen again so I am hoping this paddling will cause you to think at least twice before you do something so foolish again.

Lydia gulped through her tears, "You're going to... paddle me?"

"That's right. I'm going to spank you first until your naughty bottom is bright red, and then I'm going to paddle you with your hairbrush." He picked up the brush she had not seen on the bed next to him and wagged it in her face. She whimpered as he turned her and pushed her over his muscled right leg. She knew that being paddled with a brush would be double the pain. He positioned her so that her butt was high up in what must be perfect spanking range, and then he secured her legs with his left one. He wasted no time and began. There was no warmup. Even the first smack was strong and hard, and Lydia cried out. Cade kept up a rhythm on all parts of her bottom, sometimes smacking the same spot three or four times. She was crying hard then, but when he began to swat her upper thighs, she screamed. She had never felt anything like that before. Her butt and thighs were on fire. He stopped for a moment to scold her about willfully defying him and how this was what she could expect every time she pulled something like this. Lydia was downright bawling then, but that did not stop Cade from picking up her hairbrush to begin paddling her on top of her already blazing bottom. He smacked her with that instrument of torture over and over, and the pain had her screaming at the top of her lungs. She was pretty sure he had raised some welts with that thing.

Cade finally stopped and threw the brush across the room.

She wriggled to try to sit up but Cade still held her there, gently rubbing her back while her sobs turned to moans and hiccups.

"I'm so sorry, Cade," she blubbered. "Please don't be angry with me anymore."

"I'm not angry anymore, but we're not done here, either," he said.

"Oh, Cade, please no. My bottom is so sore!"

"That was the plan. But as I said, I want you to think seriously about this for a long time."

She felt him lean away, open a bedside drawer to take something out, and then lay a hand over her bottom. Lydia hissed at the touch but then yelped as he slid a finger along her crack and pushed in when he got to her anus.

"Cade! What are you doing?" He had never done anything like this before.

"Be still, Lydia. I can see that your bottom is red and sore on the outside but I want you to think about this for a long time. So, I am going to make you uncomfortable on the inside too."

"I don't understand," she wailed.

He smacked her very sore bottom and she stilled. He held something in front of her face that she had never seen before. It looked sort of like a baby's pacifier.

"I'm going to put this naughty girl plug into your bottom. It won't really hurt too much if you cooperate, but it will give you something to think about. You are to keep it in until I decide to take it out."

"Oh, please, Cade, no! It will hurt."

"Do as I say and the hurt will be minimal. I believe you will be more embarrassed than hurt. Now relax your bottom."

She tried, but as he moved a finger into her butt, she could not help clenching. He told her again to relax and when she didn't, he put the plug down, repositioned her and applied about ten more smacks to her swollen bottom.

"I'm sorry! I'm sorry! I'm sorry!" she cried.

Cade decided to go ahead and insert the plug quickly. It was not a large one and it wouldn't really hurt. He lubricated it and pressed up against her opening. She cried out, but when he said her name in a warning tone, she went still. When he had it fully seated, he said, "Is it hurting?"

"Um… not exactly. But I hate it. When will you take it out?" she asked through her tears.

"It will come out when I say so and not before. Mind me on this, Lydia."

He moved her to sit on his lap so he could hold her, but when she reached back to try to soothe her ravaged bottom, he said, "No. No rubbing. I want that sting to do its job of discouraging this behavior. Do you understand?"

"Yes, sir," she said as he reached for tissues to mop up her face.

Cade held her then and even though she fought it, she felt safe and protected as she pressed her face into his neck and let him rock her. And though she really didn't want to, she could feel herself becoming aroused. This had happened to her after other spankings but now the plug enhanced the jolts of desire she could feel beginning. In the last few weeks, she had just begun to deal with the fact that though she hated getting spanked, she was often aroused when it was over. She was completely dismayed to find that the added punishment of the plug seemed to also add to her need to find completion.

After holding her a little while, he reached down and pulled her panties off her ankles—the jeans had long been kicked off. Then he stood up, with her in his arms, pulled the blankets down, and laid her down on his bed.

"I'm going to get you a glass of water. I want you to drink it and take a nap."

"But it's not... I'm not—" she began to argue.

Cade interrupted her, "No buts. I need to see you have learned a lesson today, so you will stay here in bed nursing a sore and plugged bottom until I come and get you."

"Yes, Cade," she replied compliantly.

"And one more thing. Don't you even think about pleasuring yourself. You are being punished. I will be able to tell and I'll spank you every day for a week. Got it?"

"I got it," Lydia said tearfully.

He came back with a bottle of water, watched her drink some, and then tucked her in. She rolled over to sleep on her tummy and though her bottom throbbed, she surprised herself with how tired she felt. Cade checked on her after about ten minutes and found her sound asleep.

# Chapter 2

*Six weeks earlier*

W hen her twin sister and life companion left to get a master's degree in school counseling from Gallaudet–University, it was the first time they had been apart for any length of time. The twins had been even more inseparable than most, as Lola was severely hearing-impaired and Lydia was often her ears and voice. When their mother died in an accident when they were very young, they were drawn even closer.

So, Lydia had always lived in the context of her sister. They had few outside friends and neither had ever had a boyfriend. Lydia had not really contemplated life without Lola and was finding it difficult to reinvent herself without her. She was lonely and lacked confidence.

But then she was hired by a school system outside Madison to teach American Sign Language (ASL) and while she was nervous, she was also excited. She was determined to make it a success even if Lola was not with her. And from her first days working in the Three Rivers School system, she began to slowly understand that this was something she could not only do, but also do well. Her first evaluations were excellent and her confidence was building.

Now she had become a valued member of a team of professionals dedicated to facilitating the education of hearing-impaired and deaf students. She enjoyed it all, but her favorite assignments were at the high school, especially the school-to-work program. Her success with this group of students led her team to write a grant that would allow Lydia to dedicate herself full time to the school-to-work program for a one-year pilot program. So, when her principal attended their team meeting on the last day of the previous school year to tell them the grant had been funded for the following year, she was ecstatic. To top it off, her first assignment in the fall would be working with a group of six hearing-impaired young men, and one young woman, who had completed the construction tech class last year which involved helping to build an entire house. The students had developed marketable skills and were hard workers. Because she had been raised in her family's construction business and understood quite a bit about it, Lydia was the perfect fit to work closely with these students as they interned for a semester with Homes for Everyone, a program that helped to build homes for families that would otherwise not be able to own one. Lydia would work with the organization, the site foremen, and her students, to be sure they all were able to communicate at the work site.

So here they were, embarking on this new endeavor. It had been decided that the students would be introduced on site as volunteers and would work several days in that capacity. It was actually an evaluation period to see which ones were truly suited to continuing in the school-to-work program. Lydia was excited and nervous.

Cade McCauley believed in the mission of Homes for Everyone, and as a local building contractor, he and his family had donated funds and expertise to many charities' "builds". The homes built were constructed with mostly donated materials and lots of volunteer labor. The families who would eventually own the homes were taught by financial coaches about how to manage their money and by tradesmen about how to maintain a home. Without this help, these families were unlikely to ever own a home. The McCauley family's contracting business had taken the lead in the projects for many years and Cade was raised learning building skills from his father and others at Homes for Everyone sites. His great grandfather's family had started a lumber business almost a hundred years ago in forest rich south-central Wisconsin, and McCauley Brothers Lumber had evolved over time into the lumber yard and full-service contracting business. Cade and his brother Connor ran the main concern in Madison, with a smaller branch run by his uncle and cousin in central Wisconsin. They built commercial and private homes, with log homes as a specialty. The family had been very successful and his grandfather began the tradition of giving back to the community by contributing in various ways to building projects in the area. Cade really enjoyed most of the work involved in organizing these community builds and was often the lead supervisor on the projects. His younger brother Connor had, last year, begun helping him with this aspect of the business. The part of these endeavors he found sometimes frustrating was working with so many volunteers who had no idea how to even hold tools, much less use them effectively, and had to be directed and supervised. As he needed to think about liability, he had to find jobs for them that would be fairly safe, such as painting, planting, and cleaning, and still make the volunteers feel useful. It wasn't easy and required more patience than he was sometimes able to muster.

This current build had been a particularly big project. Instead of the usual three-bedroom ranch they normally built, this would be a four-to-five-bedroom home for a large family. Cade really liked the idea of a large family being given the chance to own a new and appropriately sized house. The groundwork for the house had been completed by McCauley Bros. and today was the first of four volunteer days.

He pulled up at about 7:45 and saw that there was a large group of about twenty volunteers awaiting instructions for the day and was thankful he had Conner helping him. His brother Conner had been a big help in organizing the logistics of assigning volunteers of varied skill levels to tasks that would help with the progress of the build and also help them feel productive.

Today's group was as diverse as they came, with people ranging in age from teenagers to retirees. As he scanned the group, he saw a group of teenagers who seemed to be using sign language to communicate with each other. It was then that Cade remembered that this group of deaf/hearing-impaired students had signed up to help today. He also remembered that these students might be staying on as paid interns throughout the build if they worked out. He had been in on one of the meetings about this but it was Connor who had done all the leg and paperwork. This would be something new for him. He had been told a teacher would accompany them but he did not see one.

Cade didn't know how giving directions and supervising this group would work out. He went ahead and gave general directions and rules and assigned jobs to the larger group and then made his way over to the students, to try to explain their jobs to them. He then noticed a petite young woman with a mass of thick black hair who was communicating with the students. She stood with her back to him as he approached. As he neared, he could hear her talking to the students as well as using sign language. When he got closer, she turned around and Cade found himself looking down into the most startling green eyes he had ever seen. And those eyes were the focal point of a heart-shaped face of porcelain skin, lush lips, and high cheekbones. She was quite beautiful. He was a little flustered, which was a very unfamiliar feeling for him. Before he could say anything, she held her hand out and said, "Hi! I'm Lydia Lang and these are the students from Three Rivers High School. They are anxious to get to work."

As Cade recovered some, he said, "I'm Cade McCauley, the site foreman. I was told this group would be accompanied by a teacher."

"Yes," said Lydia, laughing. "I'm their teacher. I will translate whatever you need to tell them and make sure they do as you ask. Do you have time to talk to us now?"

Again, Cade was surprised to find out this pretty young woman who didn't look any older than the students was their teacher. She was actually quite small, not standing more that 5'2".

After being instructed by Lydia to speak more slowly than he normally would, Cade led the group over to a station where there were already some volunteers—children and seniors—painting some trim pieces. "This is where I have assigned this group," he explained to Lydia. "It's pretty straightforward. Do you need some help to get going?"

"Oh, I think there has been some mistake," Lydia said. "These students have completed two hands-on construction semesters. They recently finished an entire house, learning everything from framing and flooring to plumbing and electrical work. I talked recently with Conner when I called to set up this volunteer work for them and explained their skills.

Painting trim is not for them. Do you have more challenging work? It looks like you have plenty of people painting trim."

Cade had been given a lot of responsibility in the family as the oldest boy and also in the company. This, along with his naturally dominant personality, made him unused to being challenged. This woman had completely caught him off guard.

Cade was not too anxious to hand over any power tools to these students and he had a lot of work to do still getting the day running smoothly. He was a little frustrated. "Okay," he said, "can they begin their work here and I'll send Connor over in a while to see if he can find other jobs for them to do?"

"Can we talk to Connor right now?"

Cade ran is hand through his thick brown hair and looked around for Connor. This seemed to be his problem, after all.

"Connor!" Cade barked as he motioned his brother over.

"What's up?" Connor said as he approached and took in the group of students.

Once again, Lydia stuck out her hand and introduced herself, "You must be Connor McCauley. I'm Lydia Lang, we talked on the phone about my students from Three Rivers. I believe I told you that they had construction experience, right?"

"Yes, it's nice to meet you, Miss Lang. What seems to be the problem?" Connor did remember the conversation but what stood out to him in the conversation was the fact that the students were deaf or hearing-impaired, and admittedly, he let that fact dictate what kind of job he thought they might be able to do. As Connor paused, Lydia grabbed the sleeves of both Cade and Connor and began dragging them a short way from the students. When she let go, she put her hands on her hips and started in.

"Mr. McCauley—both of you—I don't think you understand. These students are well trained and have accomplished a lot in the last year. The work you have assigned, painting trim with little kids, devalues who they are, and as you can imagine, they are often dismissed as somehow unable to do the work because they can't hear. That is absolutely not the case. I cannot ask them to spend their time today doing such unskilled work."

*Wow,* thought Cade, *this girl is a firebrand who is clearly used to being in charge.* Thoughts of the ways he could disabuse her of that notion came to his head and distracted him.

And before either man could reply, she continued, "Look, I know you are busy. I have experience with construction sites and even community builds. It looks like you need help with some framing over there and flooring in the kitchen. I could get the students started on that until you have time to assign them something else."

Now Cade was really annoyed at the attitude of this little girl. With obvious frustration, he said, "Look, Miss Lang, I apologize for my brother's mistake with an assignment for your group. He'll hunt up some tools and get them reassigned. Connor, see how they do at the framing and we'll go from there. Is that okay?"

Lydia smiled happily with a flash of white teeth. "I appreciate it, Mr. McCauley."

Without waiting for a response, Lydia spun around and walked back to her group of students. Soon, she was signing and explaining what they were going to do. Cade could not help noticing the way Lydia's jeans hugged her enticing bottom. He could not ignore thoughts of smacking that bossy bottom, and suddenly, his pants got a little tighter. He shook his head to try to clear it.

Connor began to walk off when Cade said, "Keep a close eye on them, Conn. Not sure if Little Miss Know-It-All knows what she is talking about."

Connor, who always took things more lightly than serious

Cade, was amused at the behavior of the young woman and even more amused at Cade's reaction to her. It was difficult to throw Cade off his game but this little teacher had knocked him for a loop.

"Yeah. I got this, Cade," he said as he chuckled and led the little group away.

Cade had asked Connor to keep an eye on the students, but it was Cade who kept a watchful eye on Lydia—all day. And he had to hand it to her. She had the students outfitted in safety gear in no time and then had set each one to tasks that they were completing with some competence. Lydia kept a close eye on their work and sometimes offered suggestions but never did the work for them. Her manner with the students was genuine and they seemed to like her and respect her. When they stopped for lunch, Cade watched as her hands flew in conversation with them as they often laughed together. On top of that, he was intrigued by her unusual looks and attracted by the challenge of her attitude. He would love the chance to bring that in line. Cade was impressed on several levels.

As the day wound up, Cade found that he was more relieved than usual that this was a Friday. The day had been stressful for him and he needed a break. He got busy checking on progress of volunteer groups, thanking them for their work and closing down for the night. Cade had lost track of Lydia and her group until he heard her laugh. He realized that he had heard her cheerful laugh a number of times that day and he liked the sound. He followed her voice and as he rounded a corner of the building, he found a couple of the guys who worked for him paying way too much attention to the little teacher.

"Hey, you two yahoos. There's plenty of work to do before we can go home tonight. You want to get on that?" The guys said something to Lydia and went back to work while she glared at Cade. She was pretty sure she had never met anyone as domineering and unpleasant as Cade McCauley. And she had to admit, she had never met anyone as handsome, either. She turned away from him, as a blush came to her cheeks, and went to gather up her students and get them back to school.

## Chapter 3

C ade wasn't the only one feeling relieved that it was Friday. Lydia was really tired. It had been a long time since she had spent an entire day on a building site, and this time there was the added responsibility of supervising a group of teenagers. She had been in her element today. As the ASL teacher assigned to the high schools combined with the knowledge of construction she had gleaned from growing up in a family of builders, the assignment to supervise students at a build site was perfect for her. And she would have enjoyed the day completely if not for the irritating and ungracious Mr. Cade McCauley. He and his brother would have sabotaged the work she was trying to do with the students, assuring they felt valuable at a work site despite their disability. She had found herself fighting for their rights just as she had done nearly all of her life for her twin sister.

As she changed into cozy pajamas and poured herself a glass of wine, she allowed herself to think back over the day. Lydia had to admit that the first time she laid eyes on Cade McCauley, she was shocked to realize that she found him really attractive. Who wouldn't? Cade was very tall—maybe about 6'3". He had dark brown hair that he wore longer than was fashionable. His skin was tan from outdoor work and his piercing gray eyes peered out of a rugged face. He was built like a man who did physical work for a living. Lydia had noticed in particular, his broad shoulders and narrow waist. And while she found his take charge attitude annoying, she also had to admit she found it sexy. Issuing directions and orders with his deep, gravelly voice gave Lydia a strange tingly feeling. This was new to Lydia and her independent streak could not reconcile her attraction to his masculine demeanor with her annoyance when he treated her like a bothersome child.

This was all new for Lydia who had never given boys more than a passing thought. But Cade was not a boy. He was a man—probably several years older than she was. She could not deny her attraction and had tried to catch furtive glances at him all day. And now, he was all she could think about. It was confusing because she also found him arrogant. He clearly found her to be a nuisance.

Lydia had just found her footing professionally without the attachment to her sister but was now reminded that because she had absolutely no experience with boys or men or romantic relationships of any kind, she had no frame of reference for these feelings she had developed suddenly for a man she didn't know at all. She was unsure how to handle it and her lack of confidence reared up again, making her feel inadequate and anxious. She did not want to bother Lola with her dilemma, but maybe she could talk with her only friend and coworker, Sarah. Having made that decision, she decided to watch a movie to get her mind off of Cade McCauley. Getting to sleep was difficult for Lydia that night.

She slept fitfully and finally decided to get out of bed at 6:30. Almost immediately, Lydia found herself thinking of Cade. It was Saturday and though her students would not be at the site today, she knew there would be a skeleton crew working there as well as a few volunteers. Lydia had noticed that there was only one team working on roofing. Roofing was her favorite work at a site. Her dad and brother had resisted training her but she was usually able to get her way with them. They showed her, and her twin, the rudiments of installing a roof. It struck her that if she went back to the site today, she could offer her help and maybe see Cade again.

The site was only about a mile from her apartment so she quickly ate breakfast, dressed appropriately, and walked over to the site.

Lydia thought neither of the McCauley brothers would approve of her working on the roof, so her plan was to hopefully get there before them and already be working when they arrived. When she pulled up, there were just a few people beginning work and no one was on the roof. She grabbed a utility belt and an air hammer and started up the ladder. No one stopped her, so she found the appropriate place to begin laying shingles and was concentrating on her work when she heard some loud voices. She looked down to find Cade McCauley yelling at one of his employees,

"How the hell did she get up on that roof? Did she check in with anyone?" The worker shrugged and seemed to be explaining things to Cade, but he just shook his head and made his way to stand on the ground in Lydia's view.

"Lydia Lang. What the hell are you doing? Get down from there. Now!"

---

Cade had pulled up to the site about a half hour after Lydia had begun to work on the roof. As he scanned the site, his eyes were immediately drawn to a little body perched on a high point of the roof, nailing in shingles. There was no mistaking the raven-haired bun bouncing on top of her head as she wielded the air hammer like she had done this before. As Cade had spent much of the night trying unsuccessfully to get Lydia out of his head, he had known exactly who the roofer was. Now he saw that she had stopped working and looked up but made no move toward the ladder.

"Can you get down on your own?" Cade barked. "Or do I have to come up and get you?"

"Of course, I can get down! I'll come down when I finish this box of shingles." And she went back to nailing.

Cade was livid. Not only was she directly defying him, but her dangerous position had roused an incredibly protective reaction in him.

"You'll come down right now, or I will come and get you, and you will not be happy about that!" he roared.

---

By now, Connor had wandered over to see what was going on. He took in his brother's thunderous face and the sight of Lydia's little form hunched on the roof's highest point. He couldn't help it. It struck him so funny that this young woman had his brother wound tighter than a drum and not able to control his temper. He laughed and was just about to tease his brother when Cade turned on him and yelled, "Get lost! I'll handle this!" Connor turned and walked away, shaking his head. He had rarely seen Cade like this and he believed there were going to be some fireworks when that girl finally came down to the ground. He hoped she could hold her own.

---

Cade McCauley prided himself on being in charge—at work, in his family, and in relationships with women. Yet this girl made him feel untethered. Her diminutive size and risk-taking attitude called up the naturally dominant urges he had not felt for a very long time. His lack of control over these feelings made him surly, even angry.

"Come down now!" Cade yelled again.

His highhandedness encouraged Lydia to defy him further. "No. I'll come down when I'm ready!"

With a snarl, Cade began up the ladder in a red rage. Lydia's eyes opened wide and she realized she might have pushed him too far. She nailed the last shingle and secured the hammer in her belt. She was just about to turn around to begin her descent when Cade's angry face appeared at the roofline.

"Move!" he said, clearly trying to control himself.

Lydia rolled over on her tummy and began to shimmy down the peak. She had done this many times but never with an angry bear of a man waiting for her at the ladder. She moved slowly.

Cade watched nervously, ready to grab her if she slipped. But she was moving as she should. He now had an unobstructed view of her perfectly formed bottom. He imagined that bottom stripped bare over his knee getting the spanking she deserved for this stunt. That mental picture caused him to get immediately hard. Luckily, her leg was now in reach and he grabbed it to let her know she was near the ladder.

"You're almost there. Let me guide your legs over the edge. Then I'll climb down behind you."

"I can do this all myself. Leave me alone."

"You'll do exactly as I say. Take off that belt and hand it to me so you can climb down."

Lydia unfastened the belt and handed it to him with a huff. "If you want me to come down, please move out of the way," she sassed.

She thought she heard him growl but he moved down a few rungs and waited for her.

"I'm fine," she snapped. "Keep going."

"You're not going to be fine when I get you down."

Again, Lydia felt a fissure of excitement at his pronouncement but she was also angry at his attitude. The feeling confused her and she found herself dreading having to face Cade when they hit the ground. She turned and looked up at Cade, defiantly raising her chin. Before he could say anything she said, "Look, Mr. McCauley, my family owns a building contractor and lumber wholesale business up in Green Valley. I've tagged along with my brother and dad since I was little, so I know how to do most things that need doing on a community build. I saw you only have one person working on the roof so I thought—"

"*You* thought!" he interrupted angrily. "Now you listen to me! If you know so much about builds, you'll know that the foreman is the authority here. I am the foreman. And I can tell you those who don't follow safety protocol around here are asked to leave." When her face registered shock but no words came, Cade continued, "You came here today without checking in and then took it on yourself to work on a job you are not suited for and no one asked you to do."

She realized that she *had* been little sneaky, but she did not want to back down. "But I can help. Why won't you let me prove myself?" Lydia argued as she stamped her foot on the ground.

Cade decided to act. Before she realized what was happening, she felt a huge hand grip her upper arm as he began to lead her away. "Where is your car?" Cade growled.

"I walked here. I only live a few blocks away."

With that, he changed course, and still holding her arm tightly, he began to drag her to his truck.

"Where are we going? What are you doing? Let go of me!"

He stopped, leaned in, and said menacingly, "You and I are going to have a serious discussion about who is in charge at building sites. We can have that discussion in private or right here. It's up to you." When she hesitated at the vehicle door, he barked, "Get in the truck!"

"You have no right to do this to me. Let me go! Who the fuck do you think you are?" Lydia blurted out.

"That's it!" he said as he pulled her body up against his, reached around, and administered three stinging swats to her backside. Lydia yelped and reached a hand back to protect her backside. "That kind of language is unaccept-able. Do you understand?" Her incredibly thick hair began to come loose from its messy bun and it fell down past her shoulders all the way down her back. Cade nearly gasped at the sight.

Lydia was beside herself but thought twice about respond-ing, as those swats more than got her attention. She rubbed at the sting as Cade yanked open the truck door, picked her up to deposit her in the seat, and buckled her seatbelt.

"I asked you if you understood and I expect an answer, Lydia."

She did not look up at him but just nodded.

He grabbed her chin and forced her to look at him. "Use words."

She looked up at him through thick black lashes with tears forming in her eyes and said, "Yes, sir. I understand." She didn't know where that "sir" came from. She had never said that, even to her father or brother. She worked hard not to let tears escape her eyes. Her anger was now mixed up with humiliation and trepidation. Where was he taking her? What did he mean 'serious discussion'?

Cade glanced over at the small figure who was staring out the passenger window with her arms folded over her body in a typical pout position. Now all she needed was to stick her bottom lip out—oh, there it was. Full pout. "Where do you live?"

"What do you mean? You're taking me home? I can't help today at all?"

"No. You gave up the right to work today. I want your address right now."

"Fine, you asshole. It's 211 Elmwood. It's—"

"I know where that is. And watch your language," he said as he pulled out of the yard and made a left turn. They were there in moments.

Lydia still lived in the house her father had bought for her and her sister to live in while in college. It was one of the nicer homes in the college rental neighborhood. Cade noticed that it was nicely maintained and kept up. As soon as the truck stopped, Lydia opened the door to get out.

Cade said, "Wait right there."

She obeyed with a huff and he came around to the door. As she stepped out, he grabbed her upper arm again, leading her to the door.

"Let go of me! I don't need an escort to my door!"

"Well, I say you do, and that's not all you need."

Lydia dug in her pocket for her house key and said, "I'm fine. You can go now." When he didn't let go, she looked up at his face to see an ominous twitch in his cheek.

She stopped struggling as he pulled her close, got in her face and began to scold her. "What you did today was unacceptable. It was dangerous and foolish. It's my job to keep things going and make sure everyone is safe. Your antics took a lot of my time and disrupted the entire project."

As he spoke, her expression went from anger to distress as tears welled in her eyes. Lydia was quiet for a moment and then, in a small voice, said, "I understand what you are saying. I really was only trying to help. I didn't go about it in the right way. I'm sorry. I'm really sorry."

His anger and frustration dissipated. He looked down at her for a minute, once again noticing her adorable face, and then said, "That pretty apology has saved you today. But if you ever do anything like that again, I will paddle your bottom until you can't sit for days. Do you understand me?"

Her eyes widened and as she nodded, a tear escaped down her pink cheek. Then almost regretfully, Cade turned and went back to the truck as Lydia quickly went inside so he wouldn't see her tears.

As Cade made his way back to the build site, he had the strange sensation that his life had changed in a big and unalterable way. This little troublemaker had certainly grabbed his attention. She was so little and young looking, yet she was a teacher. He wondered how old she was. Though he had been attracted to women who were somewhat submissive in the past, "little girl" looks had never appealed to him before. Was it her large, bright green eyes? Maybe it was her porcelain white skin and her curtain of jet hair? And though she was stubborn and sassy, did he detect an underlying submissive streak? Her meek "Yes, sir" and tears after being scolded were a hopeful sign. She had touched his naturally dominant personality in a way no one had for a very long time. He had found swatting Lydia's bottom very satisfying and couldn't help wondering how it would feel to have her over his knee with her jeans and panties down while he genuinely spanked her naughty bottom. Cade shook himself out of his reverie as he pulled up to the site. There were about two more hours in the day with volunteers and then he and his crew would clean up, check the work that was done, and set up for Monday. He was glad to get back to work and get his mind off one Lydia Lang.

After dropping Lydia at home, Cade cleared his head by working a few more hours, and around 3:00, he and his crew finished cleaning up and securing the site for the weekend.

When his friend Jack asked if he and Connor were going to meet them for a beer and a hot beef at The Raveno, it sounded like a good idea. He needed some distraction if he was going to stop thinking about Lydia Lang. As he thought about how her little round bottom felt as he made his point with a few swats designed to get her attention, he could feel his cock spring to life. The urge got stronger as he remembered the way she looked down with tear spiked lashes and quietly apologized afterwards. He really wondered if she had a submissive side. That was rare in young women today but his dominant side craved it. Her personality was complicated and he found himself wanting to know more about her. Damn! He had to wind down. Cade went home to shower and change then headed out about 6:00. He looked forward to that beer.

## Chapter 4

At home, Lydia was trying to straighten out her feelings for Cade McCauley. She had felt an immediate attraction to his rugged good looks and then to his unreasonably dominant attitude. She craved his attention but then hated the way he gave it in stern commands and even a swat to her bottom. Or did she hate that? She was so confused!

By the time her friend Sarah called in the afternoon to ask her out, Lydia was more than ready for the distraction of a night at their favorite bar. She needed a couple of drinks and a lot of dancing to get her mind off the enigmatic Cade McCauley. She had tried hard the rest of the day to keep busy, but her thoughts frequently strayed back to the memory of Cade's deep voice scolding her for defying him and then the feel of his powerful hand smacking her bottom. She could think of nothing else. She didn't really know much more about him. Certainly, a man that good looking already had a girl-friend, or even a wife. And even if he didn't, what made her think he would be attracted to her? He had, so far, treated her like a child! Adding to her confusion, was wondering how she could be attracted to a man like that. Hadn't she always said that she couldn't wait to get away from her protective older brother? She had no intention of ending up with a man who thought he was the boss of her. She had been on the receiving end of many spankings from her father and brother growing up and was pretty sure his wife was also subjected to the same treatment. No. She would put Cade McCauley out of her mind and have a good time tonight. Lydia showered, put on a little make up, and let her hair hang loosely—nearly to her waist. She wore her favorite pink sweater and a short, flirty, black flared skirt. With patterned black tights and short black boots, her outfit was complete. She gave herself an approving glance in the mirror. She was hell-bent on some fun.

Things started out just fine. Lydia and Sarah decided to order some famous Raveno hot beef sandwiches while sitting at the bar. Lydia found she wasn't very hungry after just a couple of bites, so she could feel a buzz from the glass of beer she had quickly gulped. The place began to fill up and a few guys at the end of the bar sent over some shots before sidling over to flirt with them.

Lydia had not thought about Cade since she got there but now could not help but compare the immature boys trying to make an impression on her to Cade's adult masculinity. One of them had singled her out and pressed her to dance, but she absolutely did not want to have anything to do with him. Sarah noticed her plight and pulled Lydia away, urging her to come with her to sing some karaoke. It was her chance to break away from Mr. Boring, but it was a tough choice, as she didn't really like getting up on a stage.

The Raveno was divided into an eating area and a stage/dancing area, connected by a large hallway displaying old photos and maps of the way the town looked long ago. Lydia could usually only be persuaded up on stage after a couple of drinks. She had only had one beer so far. Sarah, seeing her indecision and not knowing she'd had almost nothing to eat, handed her a shot and led her to stand before what was now a pretty good Saturday night crowd. The shot gave her instant confidence and when Sarah suggested they sing *Somethin' Bad* together, Lydia agreed it would be fun.

It had been a long time since she and Sarah had paired up for karaoke, but this had always been one of their favorites. She hoped she knew all the words! But once the music began and they started to sing, she remembered what a good time this was. Their harmony was pretty tight. The crowd was still noisy and paying little attention when they started so the girls felt more at ease. By the time people stopped to listen to them, Lydia and Sarah were in their groove, sounding as good as they ever had. When they finished, there was a roar of applause and after someone supplied her with another shot, Sarah easily talked Lydia into going solo with *I Try to Think About Elvis*. She had quite a bit of a buzz now and was feeling pretty good about belting out this song that was right in her range. She sensed more that saw the audience's approval as she was lost in her little world—until the song ended. As they clapped and catcalled, she made a little curtsy and looked out over the crowd to find Sarah. The place was more crowded now, and suddenly, she felt warm and a little dizzy.

---

Cade met his brother Connor and some friends for a couple of beers at the Raveno as planned. He had just begun to relax after his long day, when Connor, returning from a pit stop, said, "Hey, you should hear these girls out there doing karaoke. They're great! I think one of them might be that pretty little teacher you caught climbing on the roof."

Cade was not a fan of karaoke but followed his brother to the other side of building, where he could hear a sweet, clear voice singing a country tune. He and Connor stepped into the room to find it was pretty crowded and most of the people were actually listening to the singer who was now alone on stage. Goddammit! It *was* Lydia! She stood under a light that shone down on that magnificent head of shimmering black hair, hanging in waves around her to her waist. Her skirt was short enough to show off plenty of leg and thigh, and she wore a soft pink sweater that didn't quite cover her trim midriff. She was absolutely beautiful!

Now he pushed his way closer to the stage. Yes, there was that little troublemaker who had been wreaking havoc with his peace of mind for the last two days. He felt a now familiar twinge between his legs as he took her in. Lydia was belting out a tune and moving like a professional up there. Cade heard some guys near him talking about what they'd like to do to her. An unexpected wave of possessiveness washed over him. She seemed to be holding the attention of every guy in the audience. What was she doing wearing that scrap of a skirt and revealing top on a stage? He didn't know why, but he suddenly wanted her off that stage, out of the sight of all those men. He was surprised by the strong attraction he felt for her when he barely knew her.

Lydia finished the song to rousing applause and looked up. That's when she saw him, and he knew when she recognized him when he heard her gasp.

---

As always, when she thought of him, her confusion took over. She was embarrassed, a little angry and, she had to admit, excited. Cade towered over the rest of the crowd. He was wearing a dark gray shirt that did more to accentuate his build than hide it. The muscles in his arms were impressive and his gray eyes were piercing. She knew he had seen her, and her first thought was that she needed to get out of there. Lydia felt like she could not face him.

Her heart rate picked up. Suddenly that dizziness increased, and she felt a little unsteady. She grabbed on to the railing as she climbed off the stage. Maybe she'd had one too many shots. Damn him! Why did just the sight of him move her in this way? All she wanted to do was get to the exit. She was soon being jostled back and forth by people telling her what a great job she did. The crowd was large and her unsteadiness made it harder to maneuver. She began to feel overwhelmed and a little queasy. She put her hand up to her forehead to try to steady herself. She was afraid she might faint. Suddenly, she felt huge hands on both of her upper arms. She raised her eyes with difficulty and there was Cade McCauley, a look of concern on his face. "Are you all right?"

"I don't think so," she said just as everything went black.

Cade caught Lydia, picked her up in his arms before she could sink to the floor, and carried her out the nearest door.

The cool air outside roused her a little and she struggled to get out of his arms. "Where am I? What are you doing? I'm fine. Put me down!" She tried to sound firm, but it all came out a little breathless.

"How many drinks did you have? You are in no shape to be here. I'm taking you home," he said as he stilled her attempts to get down.

Suddenly, she cried out, "Let me down, I'm going to be sick. Please!"

Cade put her down in the grass at the edge of the parking lot and she began to wretch. He quickly grabbed her mass of hair to keep it out of the way and steadied her with his hand holding her arm. He spoke with soft comfort until she was finally finished, then he carried her to his truck where he now opened the door and reached in to get some tissues. Holding her up, he helped her wipe her mouth and face.

Lydia was pretty sure she had never been more embarrassed in her life. "Oh God, I am so sorry. I don't know what happened. I've never done this before. I guess I usually don't drink so many shots." Cade said nothing but picked her up and set her gently in his truck and reached over to buckle the belt. "What are you doing? I have to go back to my friend."

Cade's temper was just barely checked as he grabbed her chin to make her look at him. "I'll deal with your friend. What's her name? You stay right here. I mean it. If you try to get out of this truck, I will put you over my knee." He wasn't yelling, but he was clearly angry.

She nodded as he slammed the door and mumbled Sarah's name. He wasn't gone long, but Lydia had begun to feel tired and weak and had her head in her hands when he returned.

He opened the door, handed her the purse and jacket he had retrieved from Sarah, and asked gently, "Are you going to be sick again?"

" No, I don't think so, but I'm so tired."

"We'll get you home. You'll feel better soon." Though his temper was simmering, Cade knew it was pointless to take her to task while she was in this condition. It would have to wait.

Lydia rested her head against the cool window and closed her eyes. She felt so awful that she didn't even think about how she looked to Cade. She just wanted to get home to her bed.

Cade pulled in her driveway and came around to help her out of the truck. Her knees buckled and, with a curse, he picked her up and carried her to the door.

"The key is under the mat," she offered quietly.

Once inside Cade asked, "Bedroom?" and she just pointed to the hallway. He found her room and sat her gently on the bed. "Wait here," he ordered as he got a bottle of water and some aspirin. When he returned, she was already lying down with her eyes closed. He coaxed her into a sitting position. "I know you're tired, but you need to drink some water before you sleep. It will help you feel better." He handed her the bottle and two aspirin.

"Take these and drink as much water as you can, *now*," he said.

"You're so bossy," she grumbled, her speech still a little fuzzy, but she took the pills and a drink. "You can leave now. I will be okay." He ignored her and reached down to take off her shoes. "Stop it! I can do this. Leave me alone," she cried and tried to bat him away.

She tried again to lie down, but Cade pulled her to a sitting position, shoved the water at her, and said, "Drink more of this first."

She huffed indignantly but did as he said. He pulled down the covers and carefully moved her under them. Her pillow had never felt so soft and the coolness was so soothing. She wanted to sleep, but she also wanted him to leave. "Thank you for bringing me home, but I'm good now. You can go."

"I think I'll wait until your roommates get home. I'll be out on the couch."

Oh, why was he torturing her like this? "I don't have a roommate, and I'll be fine."

"You mean you live in this big house all alone?"

"My sister usually lives with me, but she is studying away this year. I'm getting used to being alone. Please go. I just want to sleep—please."

---

Cade had no intention of leaving her alone but he did not argue. He tucked her in and went out to the living room. Luckily, Lydia had a large, pit style couch and after he locked up and turned out all the lights, he found a throw and made himself as comfortable as he could. Sleep was elusive as he pictured Lydia up on stage singing her heart out in that outfit that showed all her assets. He thought about how he felt when he saw her struggling off the stage and how her soft little body felt as he held it up against his when he carried her outside. Even though he had just met her and she seemed to attract trouble, Cade realized that Lydia was special and he wanted to pursue a relationship with her. But they were going to have to get some things straight about her behavior first. Tomorrow, he would lay down the law.

## Chapter 5

Cade's phone woke him from a dead sleep at the usual time of 5:30. After he got his bearings and realized where he was, he sat up and rubbed his hand over his face. He could only have slept maybe three hours, as he was still awake when he heard Lydia get up to use the bathroom at 2:30. Well, he was awake now so he got up to check on her. He quietly pushed the door to her bedroom open and was surprised to find that she had stripped down to her panties and bra and was sprawled out on top of the covers. He couldn't help but take the opportunity to feast his eyes on what seemed to be a perfect body. Lydia had a narrow waist, with hips that flared out to greet a delicious little bottom. Her skin was so fair and looked even more so with that striking jet hair now spread out over her pillow and down her back. She took his breath away. He gently covered her with a fluffy robe she had at the end of her bed and then dragged himself back out of her bedroom before he let himself think about how it would feel to crawl into bed with her, all sleepy-soft and compliant. Compliant? So far that had not been a word he would use to describe Lydia but wouldn't it be fun taming her to it? Cade wrote her a note, left it next to the coffee maker, which he set to brew in about an hour, and went home.

---

Lydia awakened slowly to the soothing smell of coffee brewing, then sat bolt upright. How could that be? Who was making coffee? Sitting up so quickly, had caused her head to throb a bit and now memories of the night before began to come back to her. The night had begun so hopefully. She always had fun with her friend Sarah, who had picked her up, driven her to the Raveno, their favorite spot, and cajoled her into karaoke with some shots. Lydia was having a great time until she realized she had drunk too much without eating. Then she saw *him* in the crowd and it had all gone downhill. Lydia was angry about the highhanded way he had hustled her out of there and taken her home. She was also completely humiliated that she had actually passed out and then been sick in front of him. What must he think of her? She was pretty sure she had blown her chance at a date with him. Tears sprang to her eyes as she realized she might not see him again.

Lydia headed straight for the coffee machine, poured herself a cup, and took a blessed first sip. Then she noticed the note on the kitchen island.

*Lydia,*

*I slept on your couch last night, as I didn't feel you should be alone. You seemed to be sleeping just fine when I left. Do you know you snore? What you did last night was not only foolish but also dangerous, sort of like going out on a roof. I can't let that stand. You need to eat and there's not much in your fridge. I will be over later with some groceries. I expect you to answer the door.*

*Cade*

. . .

She had to admit that she was elated. He might not be happy with her, but she would see him again and maybe she could apologize. Then Lydia re-read the note. *He slept on my couch? Who does he think he is? I do not snore, and my behavior is none of his business! He expects me to just let him in so he can scold me like a kid! When hell freezes over!* She began stomping around the kitchen, slamming bread into the toaster and grabbing the jam jar out of the fridge. When the jar slipped out of her hands and crashed to the floor, spilling jam and glass over a large area, she burst into tears. What a mess she had made of everything! What more could go wrong? She was about to find out as she tried to step gingerly around the broken glass, lost her balance, and stepped on some glass pieces with her bare foot. She hopped to the bathroom, sat down, and was able to pick out most, but not all, of the pieces. She finally gave up, cleaned up the mess in the kitchen and then took a shower. Everything was more difficult now that she had a piece of elusive glass stuck in her foot. Damn Cade McCauley!

---

Cade spent the day working around his house and running a few errands like any Saturday but found he was consumed with thoughts of Lydia Lang. She definitely had a hold on him. When he saw the state of her refrigerator—one jar of pickles, two oranges, and some jam—he decided he would get her some groceries and return late in the afternoon to see that she ate and also see if he could talk some sense into her about the dangers of getting drunk in a crowded bar, or anywhere for that matter. He didn't care if she was angry about it. She was going to listen, one way or another.

Lydia felt so much better after eating a couple pieces of toast and taking a long, steamy shower. She dried her hair and moisturized her entire body, then dressed in her favorite ice blue sweats that were kitten soft and cozy. Her headache was almost gone and if she didn't stand on it, she couldn't feel the glass still embedded in her foot. She had only read a few pages in her new book when she fell asleep in her oversized chair. She must have been sleeping deeply because when the doorbell rang, she was quite startled. Was it always that loud? She slowly limped over to the door and saw through the peephole that it was Cade. She had forgotten that he said he was bringing groceries and wanted to talk with her. Well, that was not going to happen.

She yelled through the door, "Go away!"

"Dammit, Lydia. Open this door now. My arms are full."

"I didn't ask you to get groceries. Go home and take them with you."

"Look, Lydia, I know where the key is and I am coming in, either way. It will just go better for you if you open the door."

*Go better for me? What does that mean?* She hesitated, hoping he might leave the groceries and go. But suddenly, she heard the key in the door and before she could lock the deadbolt, he was standing in her doorway, looking fierce but hotter than any man had a right to. Every time she saw him, her breath hitched. His shoulders were so broad and his square jaw was covered with a little sexy stubble. His gray eyes flashed. She almost forgot to be mad as he pushed past her to put the things away in the kitchen.

"I bought some fruits, vegetables, eggs and cheese. I don't know how you live on what's in your fridge. I figured you wouldn't feel like making anything so I ordered a large veggie pizza from Sam's. Should be here in about an hour."

Lydia huffed loudly and stomped her foot, ready to demand he leave now. But her foot landed right where the glass was stuck and she let out a yelp and grabbed it, hopping to a kitchen stool. It hurt so much that tears came to her eyes.

"What is it? What happened?" In one motion, Cade threw the bags onto the table and lifted Lydia to sit on the island counter. "What's wrong with your foot? Let me see."

"No, it's nothing. Thank you for the food, but you can go now." Lydia was straining not to let her face show the pain she felt in her foot.

Cade wasn't having it. As she squirmed to get off the counter, he picked her up and repositioned her into a sitting position. Then he grabbed her wrists and got in her face. "You are going to tell me what happened to your foot. You can do it now or I can wait here all day, but you are not moving until you tell me."

Once again, the conflicting emotions of feeling embarrassed, angry, and a little aroused forced tears to her eyes. He had trapped her hands at her sides, so she took a deep breath and tried to quickly tell him what happened. "I broke a jar this morning and stepped in some of the glass. I couldn't get it all out. I think there's still some in my foot." She was speaking quickly and would not meet his eyes.

"Let me see," Cade said as he grabbed for her ankle.

"No!" she ground out and then turned to get away and reflexively kicked out at him with her good foot. Her heel accidentally connected with his jaw, hard.

She gasped and cried out, "Oh no! I'm sorry," and went still.

"That's enough," Cade roared as he put a hand to his jaw. Then he grabbed her, put his foot on the bar stool rung, and turned her over his knee all in one motion. She had to grab his ankle so she wouldn't fall and while she did that, Cade yanked down her sweats and her panties. Immediately, he lifted his hand and began to spank her bare bottom so hard, she could barely breathe.

"You are the most stubborn person I have ever known, Lydia. I am sick of arguing with you about your reckless and careless actions. That stops now!" The spanks rained down on her bottom and caused pain she had never known. How dare he do this to her?

"Stop! You have no right to do this!" she screamed and then let fly with all the obscenities she knew.

"You really want to make this worse with that language?" And he moved his huge paddle-like hand down to her thighs for a series of swats that had her screaming. "You, little girl, need a keeper! You will listen to what I tell you or you're in for a spanking—every time. I won't stop until your bottom is bright red and on fire. Do you understand?"

"Oh, please stop! It hurts!"

"Are you going to listen to me?

"Yes, yes, please, please." Lydia was desperate now and really could not take anymore. "I'll listen to you. I promise. Please stop," she wailed and went limp over his leg, not able to fight him anymore. She was out and out bawling now as she lay with her bare, well spanked and almost purple bottom trapped across his knee.

He stopped but did not immediately let her up. He kept her there to make sure his message was sinking in. After a few moments, he gently stroked her back, waited for her crying to subside some and said, "I'll let you up but you are going to let me see that foot. Do you understand?"

"Yes, sir," she blubbered. He picked her up and sat her back down on the counter. She yelped as her burning and swollen bottom contacted the hard surface. He grabbed some tissues off the table, wiped her face and made her blow her nose. She didn't argue.

When she reached to work her panties and sweats back up,

Cade said, "Just leave those right there, little girl. Having a bare bottom will help you remember to listen. You can get dressed when I say so. Now put your foot up here under the light." When she didn't immediately make a move, he said, "I have no problem continuing my discussion with your bottom but if you end up over my knee again, I'll use one of the wooden spoons you have here and that will probably add some welts to what looks to be a pretty painful area already. What's it going to be?"

Lydia turned and let him lift her foot so he could see it under the counter lamp.

"Tell me when you feel it," he said as he gently pressed her foot, looking for where the glass lay embedded. She screamed when he pressed it and tried to loosen her foot from his grasp. "I'm sorry," he said. "Try to stay still while I take a good look. I won't press anymore." More tears escaped her eyes and rolled down her face as he asked, "Do you have tweezers anywhere?"

"In the medicine cabinet in the upstairs bathroom," she mumbled. "Will it hurt?"

"Maybe for a second. It will help if you cooperate. Roll over so I can get to your foot easier." He saw her look down at her pants and panties still bunched around her knees and then up at him. "Nope. Leave them and roll over."

Even though she was mightily humiliated to have her punished bottom on view for him, she was somewhat relieved to stop sitting on it. She tried not to think about how she must look. If she thought she was confused before, she had lost her mind now. What was wrong with her that among many other feelings she was experiencing, she was also, well, turned on? How could this be? The pain and humiliation of that spanking had been extreme, but the idea that he cared enough about her to help her was unsettling. He was so domineering. She was definitely a little wet. What if he noticed? She got a headache just thinking about it.

Cade found the tweezers, some antibiotic cream, and Band-aids easily and then went to her room to find some slippers. He half expected Lydia to be up, dressed and spitting venom at him when he returned. However, the view that greeted him when he returned to the kitchen was one of the sexiest sights he had ever seen. It nearly took his breath away. There was this beautiful weeping girl lying on her tummy with her face in her hands, waves of gleaming black hair streaming down over the kitchen island, and her sore little red bottom on display, waiting compliantly for his help after a pretty severe first spanking. It was a Dom's dream. And right now, she was the picture of submissiveness. He could hope. Cade went right to work and was able to remove not just one, but three, pieces of glass from her foot before she knew it. He gently applied the cream and large Band-Aids.

"I'm putting these slippers on your feet and I want them to stay there. There may be more glass down here." He carefully placed her bunny slippers on her feet and swooped in to put an arm under her legs and carry her into the living room. He set her down on her feet and asked, "How does your foot feel?"

"Much better. Thank you." She couldn't bring herself to look up at him when she was still standing there bare bottomed and stinging.

He smiled as he reached down to pull up her pants and panties and said, "Let's get you comfortable. Sit down and put your foot up for a while." He put a pillow under her foot and went out to the kitchen. He returned with a bottle of water. "Drink this," he ordered. "I'm going to clean that kitchen floor again to make sure all the glass is gone."

By the time he came back, Lydia had rolled to her side, in deference to her bottom, he supposed, and had fallen sound asleep. As he looked down at her, Cade realized that he had some strong feelings for this woman. He found her really adorable and was intrigued by her reaction to his dominance. She had followed his commands and generally submitted to a punishment. Afterwards, she had not thrown a tantrum but had followed his directions. His hopes for a future with her were growing.

## Chapter 6

Lydia slept until the doorbell rang, and before she could even sit up, Cade had paid for the pizza and was back in the kitchen to get plates and napkins. Lydia had fallen asleep struggling with the dilemma she felt about the fact that Cade had given her a scorching spanking but then gently tended to her foot. Now he was making sure she had dinner.

He brought a tray out to her with two pieces of hot cheesy pizza and a glass of ice water. "Are you hungry?" he asked.

Lydia was so hungry now that she barely choked out a "thank you" before tucking into the pizza.

"Hey, slow down, there's plenty." He picked up his own plate and they ate in companionable silence. He noticed a couple of family pictures on the end table. He saw a girl that was certainly Lydia at about age eight or nine, with her arm around another girl who was clearly her twin sister. There was another picture with a family group—a couple, a teen-aged boy and the twins, taken at about the same time.

"Is this your family?" Cade asked.

She looked up to where he was looking and explained,

"Yes, there's my twin sister Lola and that is my brother—half-brother, really—and my dad. I told you they are part of a family lumber wholesaling business in the Upper Peninsula. My grandpa began the business seventy-five years ago and all of my dad's family helps to run it now. That's how I learned about roofing, remember?" She was smiling mischievously now.

He laughed and said, "I remember."

She looked back at the picture. "I miss my sister. She's taking a year at a different school. We've hardly ever been apart." Lydia sighed sadly.

So, his little girl was lonely. He could feel his heart ache for her, and the protective instinct he had already felt grew stronger. "My dad's first wife died after giving birth to my brother Landon. Then he met our mother. She died in a car accident when Lola and I were ten." Lydia got quiet.

"I'm sorry about your mother," he said gently.

"Thank you," she answered softly and then asked, "what about your family?"

Cade explained that he had a younger brother Connor, whom she knew. Connor and he ran the location here and his cousin and uncle ran their lumberyard and hardware store up in the central part of the state. Both of his parents were gone now.

"Do you get along with your brother?" Lydia asked but then followed with, "oh that's really none of my business. I'm sorry."

"No, that's fine. We get along great. Connor and I work together and share a lot of interests.

"That's really nice. My sister and I are really close too. I guess we're lucky," Lydia said quietly and then made a move to reach for the plates and tray to go back to the kitchen.

Cade stopped her. "No, I'll get this. You stay there. It would be best to stay off of your foot for a while."

"No. I've got to get up anyway. I have a couple of errands to run yet tonight. "

"That's not a good idea. I don't want you limping around on that foot. It will heal faster if you stay put."

"Argh! You are so high handed!"

"And you are dangerously stubborn!" he boomed. "Have you forgotten what you promised earlier?"

She considered sassing him, but her bottom was still stinging. While she considered her answer, Cade picked her up and sat her on his lap. One of his hands covered her entire butt as if to remind her what she promised. Lydia didn't really want another spanking, though she knew her body was giving other signals. She didn't have a choice. "Okay, okay! I promised I would listen to you. Now let me up, right now."

"Think about your position right now, Lydia. I have no trouble tipping you over my knee and relighting that fire on your backside. Is that what you want?"

"Of course not!" she spat.

"Let's hear that again without the sass."

Lydia gritted her teeth but did her best to seem contrite as she said, "I'm sorry I was sassy. I will listen to you."

"Then you won't be going anywhere tonight, right?"

"No, sir."

"Good girl." And with that, Cade stood up, arranging her so that they were almost toe-to-toe. He moved his hand to the back of her neck and gently moved in to kiss her.

Lydia raised her face up to greet his lips and did not resist. She had never had a kiss like that—not that she'd had much experience. His warm, full lips descended on hers and when she rose on tiptoes to meet him, his tongue boldly claimed her mouth. Lydia was overcome with desire and heard herself whimper. The kiss continued until she honestly thought she might faint.

He pulled away but kissed her face, her eyes, and finally,

the top of her head. "I've got to get out of here, Lydia, before I want to do something you are not ready for."

She wanted to scream that she was ready—please! But it was not the time. They really had only just met, and though her feelings for him were spinning out of control, she had to resist for now. He needed to go, and she wouldn't try to stop him. She kept quiet. They were still standing almost toe-to-toe and she had to crane her neck way back to look up at him.

Cade's hands still held her face. "Listen. We need to talk." He took her hand, led her back into the kitchen, then picked her up to place her back on the island counter.

"Why do you always put me here?" she asked.

"Because I want your eyes on me when we talk and you're so short that I need to sit you up here to make that happen. Also, I know you can't get away."

Lydia knew now that when he spoke sternly to her, she was aroused. She was afraid that if she looked him in the eye, he would know that about her, so she lowered her face.

He leaned toward her, gently took her chin and said, "Look at me, Lydia. I have some things to say to you." She nodded, gulped, and met his eyes. "I know we only met, what, three days ago? But I have feelings for you and I think you have some for me as well, even though I have paddled your pretty bare bottom. Am I right?"

Her eyes flashed briefly, but then she nodded.

"Okay. So, our meetings so far have not been too agreeable. But you need to know that I think you are beautiful, and smart, and fun, and I'd like to know you better. How about I cook dinner for you at my house next Friday, and we sort of begin again? Are you willing to try that?"

Lydia thought of a sassy comment but decided that she really did want to see Cade again so she said, "I'd like that."

"Good," he said as he took a step back, making her feel a little bereft. "Then I'll call you about mid-week for details." He lifted her down in front of him, and though she hoped he might want to kiss her again, he popped her nose with his finger instead and said, "See if you can stay out of trouble until then. Okay?"

She paused a moment but then answered softly, "Yes, sir."

When she locked the door behind him, she leaned up against the frame and let her feelings wash over her. Oh, that bully definitely had a hold on her already. He had taken the upper hand with her each time they were together. She would have to be very careful if she was going to maintain any independence in a relationship with him.

## Chapter 7

All day Sunday, Lydia wrestled with her thoughts of Cade. Her feelings for him were new, strong, and conflicted. As she had not had many boyfriends, actually, just the one, she didn't know if what she felt was normal or not. She sure didn't feel "normal". She was pretty sure that her experiences with Cade were out of the ordinary. After all, they had known each other just a few days, yet she felt an incredible connection. She was so very attracted to him physically, and she was shocked to find that his dominant nature caused her to feel safe, protected, and submissive. This last part was what scared her. And the spanking thing! How could she put up with that? Wasn't it abusive? She wondered if she was odd or he was perverse—or both! Was this how "normal" relationships happened? She had never heard of anything like it. She had to sort this all out before she saw him again.

So, Lydia called Sarah and asked if she could do the interpreting at the site this week while she traded places in the classroom. She needed some time away from Cade to think.

Sarah said, "Sure, I can do that. Are you having a problem or something?"

Lydia didn't know how much she wanted to share so she just said, "Not really a problem. I just have a lot on my mind right now."

"You sound a little strange. Do you want to talk? We could meet tomorrow for a bite after school at the Blue Moon."

Lydia really did need to talk this out with someone and was a little lost with her sister gone. Sarah was her best friend. Sharing with Sarah, suddenly seemed like a good idea.

"Great. I'll meet you there after school, at 5:00."

On Monday morning, Lydia regretted sending Sarah to the building site in her place almost immediately. First of all, she probably should have talked to Cade about her idea to take a break instead of surprising him by sending Sarah instead. Then, also, she preferred the work out in the field to the classroom work she had opted for and she was very anxious to see Cade again. Would he still want to take her out, or did he have second thoughts? What if he found Sarah attractive? She feared she might have made a mistake. She was so tempted to call him, but they had agreed he would get in touch with her by "mid-week" and she had to let things play out. She could wait—couldn't she?

---

When Sarah turned up with the hearing-impaired group instead of Lydia, Cade was puzzled. He had been on the lookout for their group so he greeted them just as they got out of the van. Sarah looked up at the gorgeous hunk of man who introduced himself as Cade McCauley and became a little flustered. He was even more better looking in the daylight. Really, he had movie star looks and this deep rumbly voice.

Why on earth had Lydia passed on coming back with the group today?

Cade stuck out his hand and said, "Hi, I'm Cade McCauley, foreman on this build. I believe me met the other night."

Sarah recovered and said, "Yes, I'm Sarah DiCianni. I'll be their interpreter today."

Sarah was a very pretty young woman with long blonde hair and dark brown eyes. Even though she wore overalls, a flannel shirt, and work boots just like Lydia had done, her curvy figure was evident. Cade, however, was not interested and looked around her thinking that Lydia might still be in the van.

Sarah noticed and said, "Um, Lydia won't be here this week. She's helping out in a couple of classrooms. I think I can do the job, though."

"Oh, I'm sure you can," said Cade who could not hide his surprise at this turn of events. "Let me get my brother Connor. He'll help supervise your group today."

Cade called Connor over and made introductions, noticing the way Sarah and Connor smiled at each other.

"You've got a plan for them today, right?" Cade said gruffly.

"Yeah, big brother, I'm on it. No worries. Follow me, everybody."

Cade watched Sarah walking away and then sign to her students and share something with Connor that made him laugh. Where the hell was Lydia? He was concerned. Maybe she'd had second thoughts after he spanked her. But then she had seemed fine after they ate dinner and seemed ready to go out with him this coming Friday. Then he got angry. If she had concerns, she should have talked with him instead of just not showing up. That was childish. On the other hand, the short time they'd known each other had not been what a girl like Lydia would consider romantic. On the contrary, their time together could be called intense. He might have scared her off with his overbearing nature. Cade found himself at a loss with a woman for the first time ever and spent the morning struggling to focus on the job at hand. Damn that Lydia Lang!

At lunch, Cade noticed Connor sitting with the pretty teacher and the students. Was Connor putting the moves on her? He walked over and interrupted, "I'm sorry to bother you during lunch but can I talk to you, Ms. DiCianni?"

Connor was not happy. "She just began eating, can't it wait?"

"No. It can't. Why don't you take a few minutes and check in with the other volunteer groups?"

Cade could tell that Connor was annoyed, but he met his glare with one of his own and stomped off.

"Sarah, I'd like to thank you for your help today. The students here do a really good job but it couldn't work without you, or Lydia."

"Thank you," she said, smiling, and he noticed she had two dimples framing full, lush lips. No wonder Connor was interested. But Cade only had his raven-haired troublemaker on his mind. What game was she playing? If she were here right now, he would march her into the trailer and swat her bottom until she told him what she was up to. Damn, if that thought didn't set his cock twitching.

"What happened that Miss Lang didn't come with the students today?"

---

*Oh,* Sarah thought, *Lydia has definitely gotten the attention of this unbelievably good-looking foreman.*

"I'm not really sure, but yesterday she called and asked me

to switch assignments with her for this week. We share ASL responsibilities, but I am nearly always in the classrooms while Lydia is usually out at work sites. I was happy for the chance to come today and I'm having a great time." Then something occurred to her and she bit her lip. "Are you unhappy with our group or my work today?"

"No, of course not. It's just that I thought Miss Lang was pretty comfortable on the site last week, as she knows about construction and, of course, knows the students."

"Yes, her family owns a contracting business in the Upper Peninsula, I think, so she was raised doing this stuff. I don't know much about it, but I can interpret directions well and Connor is such a big help."

"I'll bet he is," Cade said as he scanned the site to see where Connor had gone. "Well, again, thanks for your help, and please, if you see Miss Lang, tell her hello."

"Yes, sir, Mr. McCauley."

As Sarah made her way back to the students, she was thinking that she couldn't wait to see Lydia tonight. She was sure she had not heard the whole story about Cade McCauley.

## Chapter 8

Lydia's Monday seemed to stretch on forever. She had a terrible time focusing on her work in the math classroom to which she had been assigned. She pictured Cade working at the site, barking directions to workers while his muscled frame was barely contained in work clothes. He was so hot! Then her mind wandered to all he had done with her in the last week—his stern scolding, his sexy kisses, even that awful spanking. She had to admit that thoughts of his masculinity fired her panties all day. She had to force herself back to reality several times and ended up really feeling frustrated. If she were honest, she was regretful that she hadn't just gone to the site with the students so she could work near him again.

By the time she met Sarah at the Blue Moon, she was frazzled. She considered guzzling a beer while she waited but remembered Cade's reaction to her drinking and ordered a soda. Sarah raced in about ten minutes late. She was windblown and had rosy cheeks from working outside all day. She also seemed quite excited. Lydia waved Sarah over to the bar stool next to her.

Sarah threw her coat and purse on the stool next to Lydia and said breathlessly, "God, Lydia, why didn't you tell me about the hot 'brothers McCauley'? Those guys are so good looking and I love the way Connor works with the students. I had such a fun day! How come you wanted to trade with me?"

Lydia looked at Sarah, wide-eyed. It had never occurred to her that Sarah would be impressed with Cade or interested in Connor, but who wouldn't be? "Well, it's kind of a long—and personal story," said Lydia.

"I've got the time. Come on; spill it! Did something happen between you and Cade? He asked me about you today. I think he's really interested in you, Lydia. What happened last week?"

Lydia paused and said, "Let's get a pizza and move to a booth; we need privacy." When they got resettled, she wondered again if she could talk to Sarah about this. But then she took in Sarah's truly caring look and remembered that she was her best friend. And Lydia really needed someone to talk to about Cade. So, she began to tell Sarah about meeting Cade at the site, her little adventure up on the roof the next day, the glass in her foot, and the mind-boggling kisses. She left out the parts about the spankings and other embarrassing events.

"Oh my God! All of that happened in just the last few days? That's amazing!" She paused and said, "You know when he talked about you today, he got this look. I think he is more than interested. It seems like you had sort of an explosive beginning. Are you trying to back up and take a break? I could understand that."

Sarah seemed to completely "get" Lydia's feelings. No wonder they were such good friends. Lydia nodded.

Sarah continued, "I've got to tell you that his brother Connor caught my eye. He is also so sexy and I love how easy going he is. I talked with him some, and I can't wait to go back tomorrow."

Lydia was surprised about Sarah and Connor and asked her all about her day with him. It did seem like there was a little spark there. Wow! What a coincidence.

As the girls ate, Lydia grew quiet.

Sarah said, "What's up? I don't think you are telling me everything. You don't have to if you don't want, but I'm here to listen. Have you got a real thing for Cade?"

Lydia finally succumbed to the temptation to tell Sarah all about her conflicted feelings about Cade. She told her how her feelings for him had gone from zero to sixty in the short time they had known each other, but then how she had made him angry enough to actually spank her. Sarah was a good listener and when she didn't appear shocked, she also told Sarah what Cade had said about being in charge and about how he felt about spanking. By the time she was finished, her face was bright red and she couldn't even make eye contact with Sarah.

But Sarah was smiling kindly. "I see," she said. "You want to let yourself like him but you're conflicted about his Neanderthal ways. Am I right?"

"Oh, Sarah!" she said, relieved. "That's it exactly! How can it be that a man in these times thinks this is okay? But worse, how can I find it so sexy? I mean, that spanking hurt like crazy and was so humiliating. I hated it! But the words he used when he threatened to spank me and then the way he scolded me during—I just melted like a little fool. And when he finished up by comforting me in his arms, I actually lost all sense of time. What in the world is wrong with me?"

"Lydia, really, did you not know that erotic spanking is a thing? Lots of couples role play daddy/little girl or master/slave."

"Ew! No, I never heard of that and that is just perverse.

Besides, Cade's spanking was not erotic; it was a punishment. It's true he calls me 'baby' and 'little girl' but that has nothing to do with it!"

"Ah, it sounds like he may be a Dom. Do you think you might be a little submissive?" Sarah asked.

"I don't know. I never considered it. Is that a thing too?" Lydia was incredulous.

"Oh, Lydia. You are so innocent—and adorable! And, yes, there is a difference between erotic spankings and punishment spankings, but I think the effect is nearly the same."

"How do you know so much about all of this?" she asked, a little defensively.

"Oh, I was raised in a family where my dad was the head of the household. That didn't mean he ordered my mom around or she did whatever he wanted all the time—but they didn't always agree, and in the end, my dad was in charge."

Shocked, Lydia asked, "Did your dad spank your mom?"

"I never saw it, but as I got older, I noticed some signs and heard them talk so that I figured out what was happening. When my older brothers got married, I knew they spanked their wives because my sisters-in-law worried about it and talked about it. I never saw it happen, but I heard it happening a few times."

Lydia couldn't say anything. This was a lot to take in. "Will you allow a man to spank you when you get married?" she finally asked.

"I was spanked plenty as a child and I swore that I would never marry someone who thought they could upend me to spank whenever they wanted. But one day, after my sister-in-law had been spanked, I asked her why she married my brother if she knew he was such a caveman. And wasn't it abuse?"

"What did she say?" Lydia really wanted to know.

"She said she loved him. And his dominant way was part

of him and part of why she loved him. She said a spanking was not at all the same as abuse and while her bottom might be sore for a few hours and her dignity knocked down a few pegs, things were always better afterwards. She told me that she felt loved and protected when my brother cared enough about her health and safety to take her in hand. Besides, she said he was not going to change and that was part of the man she loved. So, will I ever marry someone who spanks me? I don't know. I still would rather find a guy who doesn't, but it's not a deal breaker."

Lydia had a thoughtful look on her face. "Wow, Sarah, you've given me a lot to think about. I am still a little confused, but you answered a lot of questions. Thanks! Thanks for everything," she said as she stood and gave Sarah a hug.

As Lydia drove home that night, her head felt ready to explode, but the more she thought about Cade, the more she wanted to give a relationship a chance. There was just so much to work out. How did he view their relationship? Was she just a passing fling with a naïve young woman with whom he would soon be tired? Or was there more? Was he truly dominant? And what did that mean for his expectations from her? And if they did want to pursue a relationship, how could they maintain their professional lives in that context? And lastly, was she overthinking it like she did with most things? Sarah had helped her sort out some of the issues, but there was so much more.

## Chapter 9

When Sarah returned to the site, instead of Lydia, on Tuesday and Wednesday, Cade went from disappointed to angry. He understood that they had gotten off to a rocky start and that Lydia needed some time to process her feelings, but he thought a couple of days would do it. If it was such a big dilemma, then he wanted to talk to her about it but was still hesitant to call her. She might resist being pushed. As the days progressed, he became more sullen. He stomped around the building site growling at everyone, especially Connor. It didn't help when he saw Sarah and Connor talking and laughing together all day.

By Wednesday afternoon, Connor had just about had it when Cade snapped at him for something that was not his fault. "Hey!" He turned angrily to Cade. "I don't know what's gotten into you the last couple of days, but you have been a jerk—to everyone. Cut it out! If this is about Lydia, then go ahead and handle it, but don't go around finding fault with everyone because things aren't going your way with a woman."

Cade's face turned thunderous and he took a step toward

Connor in confrontation. But Connor had dealt with his older brother all of his life and knew he didn't need to back down. They stared at each other for a few moments and finally Cade said, "Yeah. You're right. I'm sorry. I'll handle things."

"Great!" replied Connor as he began to get back to work. Then he stopped and said, "Hey, Cade. Maybe soften up a little before you "handle" things. Some flowers might be a good idea."

Cade rolled his eyes. He decided right then that little Lydia Lang had yanked him around enough. He couldn't think clearly about anything else. Thoughts of her jet-black hair against her soft white skin, her lush lips waiting for a kiss, her pert little bottom turning pink under his hand, consumed him. Cade felt a real need to be with her. If she decided he would need to tone down his domineering personality in order to be with her, he might consider it, so smitten was he with that girl. He would talk with her tonight, come hell or high water.

In the meantime, Lydia had come home from school feeling completely stressed. She no longer enjoyed working in the regular classroom setting as much. The school-to-work program was so much more fulfilling. And more importantly, dragging her thoughts away from Cade McCauley took a lot of effort. Memories of the few days she had spent in the company of the heart-stopping, handsome man who paid such close attention and care to everything she said and did, was playing on a loop in her head. She could hear his stern voice scolding her and feel his hands embracing and then spanking her. After her eye-opening talk with Sarah, Lydia thought about how she might be able to work it out with Cade after all. She was certain she did not want to give him up. She poured herself a glass of wine to wind down and think. She wished yet again that he would call, and then, as if on cue, her phone rang. The timing caused her to gasp so when she answered, she was a little breathless.

"Lydia. Are you all right?" Cade asked when he noticed her breathing.

"Yes. I'm fine, but I was just thinking about you and it surprised me to see your call."

Cade was happy to hear her voice but ignoring his brother's advice to go soft, he barged right in. "I'm making dinner here at my house tonight and I want you here. We have a lot to talk about," he all but commanded.

Lydia was thrilled that he had called and had really wanted to talk with him, but his manner put her on the defensive. "I don't know, Cade, it's sort of late notice and I don't even know where you live."

"That's why I'll pick you up in an hour. We really need to talk."

No asking—just telling! She was nervous about calling him on it, but it seemed important to begin as she meant to go on. "Are you asking me or telling me, Cade McCauley? Honestly, you are so... so... unromantic. I don't think I want to see you tonight," she said angrily, and he thought he heard her voice hitch.

Damn it! What was he doing? This was *not* the way to approach her now. "Lydia. Look, I'm sorry. You're right." He paused and began again, "I have missed you this week and would really like to make dinner for you tonight. I know it's last minute, but I am hoping you will consider it. I'd be happy to pick you up—whenever you can be ready."

Lydia was quiet so long that he worried she might have

hung up, but then he heard her say, "I'd really like to have dinner with you tonight, but I can drive myself."

"No!" he said gruffly and then caught himself. "I mean, I would really like to pick you up, please."

She paused, "Okay, I can be ready at 5:30. Does that work out?"

"Great! I'll see you soon."

---

Lydia realized that call had made her so happy. He must have missed her almost as much as she missed him. He wouldn't pick her up and cook her dinner if he wanted to call things off. She was relieved and excited. She knew now that no matter what, she would find a way to make Cade's dominant personality work for her life. She had not experienced love before, but what she felt for him was very powerful. Maybe this was it. But wait, what was she going to say? 'Oh, yes, Cade, I will do whatever you say and will accept that you will spank me when I don't?' Of course not! Yet she knew she couldn't ask him to change, so she would have to come to an agreement they could both accept. She would do her best.

She had just forty-five minutes to change from after-school-tired to seductive siren. She decided to soak a bit in a scented bath, piling her hair on top of her head, as she had no time to wash and dry it all. Applying lightly fragranced body lotion *all* over, she felt as sexy as she could at the end of the day. With just fifteen more minutes until he arrived, she raced around dressing in one of her favorite soft, form fitting sweaters. She paired that with a pair of black leggings that hugged her body perfectly. Lydia never wore much make up so she just touched up with some mascara, a lip-gloss, and light blush. She brushed her hair upside down to give it as much shine and volume as possible and before she could check herself out in the mirror, the doorbell rang. She ran to open it and stopped herself just before she threw it open. Taking a deep breath to calm herself, she opened the door to find Cade smiling at her. How could he be more good looking than she remembered? But he was! Really, her heart nearly stopped as she looked up at his still-wet hair and day's-growth-covered face. He wore a buttery brown leather jacket over a gray Henley and jeans that showed off his muscular legs and perfect butt.

"Hi! Come on in. I'm almost ready."

---

Cade watched her sit down and put short red boots on her tiny feet then race to find her bag and coat. He found her adorable. She was more than adorable, really.

She looked—well, delicious. He didn't know if he could stop himself from ravishing her right then and there. They had a ways to go in figuring each other out, but he was getting more and more impatient. And tonight, was just the beginning.

"You look great, Miss Lang—and you smell good too."

She dazzled him with a smile and said, "You clean up pretty nicely yourself, Mr. McCauley."

He helped her with her coat and led her out to the truck where he lifted her up into the seat and fastened the seatbelt. As he got behind the wheel, he had to admit that he was a little nervous. What if she had thought about him and decided not to pursue a relationship? Well, there was only one way to find out.

## Chapter 10

Cade's house was about thirty minutes away, in what Lydia would call "the country". His driveway was long and led to a beautiful log, multi-level house surrounded by trees and shrubs. The landscaping looked planned but natural. Outdoor lights made it look welcoming.

Lydia was impressed. "Oh, Cade, what a great place," she said sincerely.

"Thank you. I built it with my brother, uncles, and cousin, about five years ago."

Cade looked over to see her taking in his property with that bright smile and sparkling eyes. She fairly bounced with enthusiasm, reminding him of a little kid. As he watched her, he wondered if there was a more beautiful girl anywhere.

He parked in the driveway, as he wanted to take her in the front door. He stopped the truck and said, "Wait there."

Lydia was so excited, she didn't hear him at all. She unfastened the seatbelt, threw open the door and began to jump out just as Cade came around the front of the truck.

"I told you to wait, right?" he asked sternly.

She was embarrassed as she replied softly, "Right. I'm sorry."

"This truck's cab sits high, and you could hurt yourself jumping out without thinking—as you were clearly going to do. I don't give directions just to hear myself talk. There is always a reason and I expect you to listen better. Do you understand?"

Lydia nodded and looked up at him through her thick lashes, gaging his mood. I understand," she said, though she shivered a bit from the cold.

"Come on. Let's get you inside."

He opened the front double door, and the great room that was laid out in front of her stunned Lydia. "Oh, Cade! This is magnificent. I love everything about it. The two-story windows and the way you can see all the rooms around the great room!" She ran over to the huge fireplace. "And this hearth, it's just so welcoming. And it's decorated so tastefully. Did you do this?"

Cade was charmed by her bubbly reaction. "We have a decorator and a stager who rents space in our office and helps us out getting properties ready to see. She helped me a little."

"Can you show me everything?" she said as she began to wriggle out of her coat.

"Hey! Settle down," he said as he helped her with her coat and hung it up. When he turned around, she was already in the kitchen.

"Wow! Cade, this is a chef's kitchen. Are you a good cook?"

"Hardly a 'good' one, but I can manage."

"Forgive me for saying so, but this is such a big house for you—well, not for you because you're pretty big, but for one person." Lydia twirled around the kitchen with her arms out, indicating space. Her delight made him smile.

"I built this house to be my forever home. I hope to build

my future here so I designed everything the way I wanted it to be forever. I'm pretty happy with it."

Lydia grabbed his hand and tried to lead him down a hall. "Show me more!"

Cade tugged her to a stop and lifted her up to sit on the kitchen counter. "Hey, I said settle down." He raised one eyebrow and lowered his chin in a no-nonsense kind of way. "I'll show you the whole place. Just let me get some of the food out and get you something to drink first. Wine?"

Chastened, Lydia said, "Yes, please," and sat quietly, watching him bring some steaks, twice baked potatoes, and salads out of the fridge.

"That looks wonderful," she said, though she would never be able to eat all of it.

"I'll just heat the potatoes through while the steaks are on the grill. Here's that wine. Let's take it over to the fireplace. Are you cold?"

"A little," she admitted as she hopped off the counter. Lydia wondered if the vibrations she felt were from cold or desire. She watched Cade's muscles ripple through his shirt as he put some logs on the fire and then lit it.

He went back to the kitchen and brought out some snacks and signaled her to sit. She chose to sit cross-legged on the enormous ottoman directly in front of the fire.

"Comfortable?" he asked.

"I feel just wonderful," she said as she watched him sit on the edge of the sofa facing her. Then he took her wineglass, put it down next to his and took her hands in his.

She blushed a little and said, "This seems pretty serious, Cade."

"It is," he said, and when she began to say something, he put a finger on her lips. "Listen, Lydia. I have some things to say to you, and I want you to just listen. Got it?"

When she nodded, he said, "Use words please."

"Yes, sir," she said.

"Good girl."

When he talked to her in that way, she felt a tingling run through the very center of her. It was a little unnerving.

"Lydia, I believe in honesty and transparency—always. So, I need to tell you how I feel. Since the first time I saw you, I thought everything about you was special—your looks, your ability to teach and communicate with students, and the fact that you don't mind working hard. I think you are fun and sweet. I've never met anyone like you. I feel like I've known you always."

Lydia was stunned, both by the way he felt about her and that he would come out and tell her. She was so touched that tears pricked her eyes. It took her a moment to recover. But then she said, "Oh, Cade, that is the nicest thing anyone has ever said to me. I am touched." A tear slipped down her cheek and he wiped it away with his thumb.

She struggled with what to say to him. "Cade, I know you like honesty, and I do too. but… but…"

"What is it, baby?"

She went all soft inside when he called her that, but she forged ahead. "I just don't understand why a guy like you would be interested in me? You have so much going for you. You own this beautiful home and run a business. And I think you are, well, so handsome. Really, sometimes when I see you, my heart nearly stops. You must have women after you all the time. Why would you choose me? It frightens me."

"What?" he said too loudly. "What do you mean, it frightens you? I don't understand!" He seemed angry, but she had to continue.

"I am afraid that my feelings will get too… will be too much… oh! I'm afraid that I'll fall in love with you and then you will get tired of me and find someone else." Tears began then as she added, "I'm sorry, but you wanted me to be honest. I'm trying to be."

Cade was moved by her honest and innocent revelations. He reached forward and put his hands on the sides of her face. "Okay, little love, I appreciate your honest transparency. I can't imagine ever getting tired of you."

With that, he reached in, pulled her to him, and slanted his lips over hers in an all-consuming kiss. When his tongue began to explore her mouth, she followed his lead and responded. By the time he pulled away, she was short of breath. Then he surprised her by putting his hands around her tiny waist and positioning her to face him. Her legs were spread over his and his hands held her upper arms. She looked at him, puzzled, when he gave her a little shake and said, "Listen to me. This bit about why I would fall for 'little old you' or that I would ever hurt you—I don't ever want to hear it again! I want this relationship to grow and hopefully be exclusive and permanent. We need time to know each other more, but that is what I see for us. And one more thing, I will not put up with you putting yourself down or having doubts about yourself that get in the way."

When she was quiet, he shook her gently again. "Do you understand me?"

"Yes, sir. I'll try," she replied quietly.

"You'll do more than try. What do you think will happen to you if you don't do as I say?" He let one of his huge hands move to cover her bottom and gently patted it.

Her knees were still positioned on the outside of his muscular thighs and while she felt vulnerable, she also had never felt so safe. But she didn't want to answer him and lowered her eyes to avoid the question.

"Answer me, Lydia. What will happen if you don't mind me?"

She blushed furiously and began, "You will... or I will get..."

Cade patted her bottom a little harder and waited.

"I think you will spank me," she blurted out as fast as she could, staring down at her hands.

"You bet I will. I will turn you over my knee, bare your bottom, and keep spanking or paddling this little butt until it's bright red and raw. And if you're extra naughty, I'll stand you in the corner so that sore bottom will be on display until I think you have learned your lesson. Do you understand?"

She gulped and said, "Yes, sir."

"I mean it, baby. Don't test me."

"No, sir."

His stern words and her vulnerable position caused her panties to get more than damp. She was paralyzed with worry that he would notice.

Cade knew that if he didn't stop now, he would lose control, so he said, "Hey, I told you I would make you dinner. Are you hungry?" He got up and headed for the kitchen.

*Hungry for you*, thought Lydia, but she said, "Sure. Can I help?"

Lydia needed some time to process the things he told her and to do something about the fact that she was positively vibrating with need for him. She was trying to manage lots of "big feelings". She felt excited, hopeful, and on the edge of something important.

## Chapter 11

Cade served a mouth-watering meal. The steak was just like Lydia liked it and the potatoes were big and flavorful. Lydia was complimentary but grew quiet as they ate.

Cade noticed her silence. "Are you finished, baby?" he asked.

"Everything was wonderful, Cade, but I just can't eat any more."

"Sure, let me get you some coffee and we can sit by the fire."

Lydia began to clean up but he told her to leave it. He knew they needed to talk more.

Lydia took off her shoes and sat in the corner of his plush sectional. She curled her legs under her and snuggled next to a soft, warm throw. That's how Cade found her as he brought her coffee out.

"You look comfortable," he said.

"Oh, Cade, this is the most wonderful home. I don't know how you ever leave it. It's beautiful, peaceful, and cozy. I just love it."

He came to sit in front of her, facing her on the large ottoman, and put down his coffee mug. "I'm really happy you like it here. I hope you'll spend lots of time in front of this fireplace," he said, looking directly into her eyes. "I need to tell you that when you didn't show up on Monday at the site, I was really disappointed—and worried too. I knew you needed some space, but we didn't talk about Sarah coming in your place. Why didn't you talk to me about that?"

Lydia was quiet while she thought. Then she said, "I have thought and thought about how to pursue our relationship while also maintaining our professionalism at work. It's really a dilemma."

"I don't know, Lydia, there are lots of workplace romances that seem to work out."

"I know, but our situation is different—more complicated."

"What do you mean?"

"Well, I'm a teacher working with students who watch what I say and how I behave all day. I need to be a shining example in all ways. You and I would have to be more than proper. And I think they would suspect something right away. I wouldn't want to keep secrets. And then there are some of the guys on the site. I know you've talked with them about their language in front of the students but I would be mortified if the kids ever overheard any gossip or crude talk about us. That's why I switched with Sarah. I had hoped I could figure it out—but I can't. And I really want to be back working on the build. I don't know what to do." Tears were forming in her eyes and she was wringing her hands.

She looked so tiny nestled in the corner of his huge sectional. He could see she was upset, so he resolved to calm her fears. Cade took her coffee mug, set it aside, and lifted her into his lap. He rocked gently and said, "You've got yourself pretty worked up about this, don't you?"

She nodded miserably.

"I want you onsite as well, so we have to figure something out. First of all, I know you don't know me well yet—which I think is part of the problem. I would never embarrass you or let anyone else do so, either. I think you'll find that I'm a little old fashioned, so I will be discreet and polite. I also insist that my crew behaves appropriately. He turned her in his lap so she was facing him again. "Do you think you can trust me?"

Lydia looked at his handsome face that was now serious and sincere. She believed she could trust him to make this work.

"I also think that while our... friendship does not need to be announced, it also doesn't need to be a secret. We are not doing anything wrong. How do you feel about that?"

"Well, I'm thinking about what my program director would think about us. I think if I talked to him about it up front, it would be okay. I hope so," she said as she bit her lip. "You know, Cade, the execution of this grant is so important to the future of the school-to-work program and I feel so responsible. I may be overthinking things, huh?"

"Maybe, but I think they don't know what they have in you, Lydia," Cade said as he touched the side of her face affectionately. "You are so dedicated to the success of the program and to the kids. And you are good at what you do."

Lydia blushed with pleasure at the compliments and said, "Thank you."

"Are you feeling better about things now? Do you think you will be ready to come back on Monday?"

"I do," she said confidently. "Cade, thanks for helping me with this. You know I have been overwhelmed by so many feelings in the last week. I am anxious for the students to succeed as well as the program and then there's... well, there's you," she said, peeking up at him.

"Me? Whatever do you mean, Ms. Lang?"

"Well, you're a lot to take in, Mr. McCauley."

"Go on," he said, looking interested.

"Okay, I'll just tell you the truth."

"Best place to start," he said with a smile.

"But you have to promise not to tease me or make fun of me," she said with a little pout.

"Never," he said seriously while placing her back on the sectional to face him. "Tell me why I'm a lot to 'take in'."

Lydia was nervous about baring her soul to him but she had always found that being honest was best. If he didn't like what she said or thought she was just a foolish young girl, better that she know it now before she could get hurt badly if everything ended.

"When I first saw you, I was sort of miffed at where the students had been placed, remember?

"I do," he said, trying not to smile as he remembered her little form standing with her hands on her hips taking him and Connor to task for not respecting the skills of her students.

"I was sort of mad, but when I saw you, I felt... I thought... oh, Cade, I thought you were the handsomest man I had ever seen. I think I even stopped breathing for a minute, and I had to concentrate hard on what I was saying."

Lydia's face was now in sort of a permanent light blush that Cade found as charming as her honesty. She was really so innocent. Cade said nothing but continued to listen.

"Then, the next day, when you got angry with me for going out onto the roof, I wanted not to like you." And now she looked directly at him. "You are very bossy, Cade."

"Uh huh," he said, and then, "you wanted not to like me but..."

"Yes. But when you talked to me like that, I realized it made me feel safe and cared for, and also it made me feel sort of... oh, this is difficult."

"Sort of turned on?" he offered.

Now her blush was full blown and she hid her face in her

hands. "Yes! And I don't know why. I should have been mad at you for taking me home and threatening to spank me. And I was, but I had conflicted feelings and I don't know what's wrong with me. I've never felt this way before." Lydia was agitated now. "What must you think of me?"

There was not much Lydia could have said that would have pleased Cade more. She was describing the feelings of a submissive. Young women like her, who could complement his dominant traits, were few and far between, and he could not believe his luck finding one like Lydia. But she was so young and naïve. He would have to explain things to her in a way that didn't scare her. He was a little nervous. If he didn't handle this right, she could walk away.

Before she could continue, he leaned forward, put his hand behind her neck and drew her in for a powerful kiss. When he pulled away, he said, "I've told you that I think very highly of you. The fact that you are submissive just adds to the list of qualities I find so beautiful about you. You do *not* have to feel badly about those feelings. They are natural for you and make me very happy."

Lydia bit her lip as she processed this information. "But I don't want you to think I enjoy your spankings. I don't! And I don't know if it's okay for me to... allow you to do it."

Cade smiled gently and said, "You've had a lot on your mind, haven't you? Let me tell you where I'm coming from and how I like to handle things." He sat forward, took her hands in his and began, "It's in my nature to be take charge and protective. It's the way I'm made. In a relationship, I can handle some give and take and I will always listen to your side of things, but in the end, I have to be the one who makes the decisions and who holds you to a standard of behavior, especially as it pertains to your health and safety." Lydia tried to remove her hands from his, but he held firm, saying, "Please sit still, look at me, and hear me out."

Lydia raised her eyes to his with some trepidation. "Okay, go on."

"You know that my preferred way to resolve disagreements is to bare your bottom, put you over my knee and spank you until you see the light. Do you understand?"

Lydia's face clouded over at his proclamation that he believed spanking her was completely acceptable. And she couldn't believe he would come right out and say it! "What I understand is that I don't like that you think you have the right to scold and spank me like a child whenever you think I deserve it. It really hurts and I want you to promise never to do it again—and let go of me!" she said as she tried again to extract her hands from his grip.

Cade did not let go but continued calmly, "When I spank you, it's because I think you are acting like a child, and I understand that it hurts. That's the point. A spanking or paddling doesn't do any lasting damage but can deter the receiver from repeating a poor decision. And if my memory serves, you have made a couple of bad choices in the short time I have known you."

"Oh, do you have a lot of experience spanking women?" she said with a little lip.

"Enough," he snapped, then sighing, he said, "Look, Lydia, I am trying to lay my cards on the table here before we go any further. I've told you how I feel. Maybe you should take a few days to think about where you want this to go. But know that I hope you will want to continue seeing me and in fact, be mine. What do you think?"

Lydia sighed. "I think I do need some more time to think about it. We moved sort of quickly." When he said nothing, she continued, "Now, more than ever, I think it's better if Sarah takes my place on site for the rest of this week, and we take a break. I can come back on Monday if things work out.

Sarah is enjoying it and I think she is enjoying Connor too," she said as she smiled mischievously.

"I think you're right. Connor's head is in the clouds when she is around. They seem to get along."

Cade noticed that Lydia had yawned a few times now, so he said, "Come on, baby, let's get you home. You're tired."

"But we have to clean up," she said as she shot up and headed for the kitchen.

"Stop!" said Cade as he stood. "Come here."

She stopped and looked up at him feeling unsure.

"I said come here," he said again.

She slowly walked toward him. When she got close enough, he grabbed her with one arm and used the other hand to raise her chin to look at him. "I think we got some things worked out tonight, right? But you're tired. It's late. You're going home to bed. I can clean up just as quickly without you. Put on your shoes while I get your coat."

Lydia felt strangely bereft when Cade moved away from her. Her body told her she was ready for more, but her brain insisted on thinking it through. Cade put her in the truck and as soon as it heated up, she fell asleep.

## Chapter 12

While Sarah took Lydia's place at the Home for Everyone site, Lydia was assigned to the early childhood center for the rest of the week. She really loved working with three-and four-year-olds, and if she couldn't be at the work site, that was certainly second best.

She knew most of the teachers and assistants at the preschool and was happy to be there. The days were filled with activity, not leaving her too much time to think about Cade.

But as soon as she got in the car to go home, her head filled with longing to see and hear him again. While they had only known each other a short time, their time together had been life changing. She felt more and more that what she felt for Cade was love, so the idea of 'taking a few days' to consider going forward was painful. There were so many things to love about him. He was movie star handsome, intelligent, and successful. He was also hard working and kind. Really, he was just about everything a woman could want. But his dominant tendencies and old-fashioned idea that it was okay to spank her if he thought she was endangering her health or safety, gave her pause. He had told her his feelings honestly and said it was the way he was and there would be no changing. The spanking and few random swats she had received from him didn't make her afraid but she sure hated the pain and humiliation they caused. And perhaps her biggest dilemma was that when he spoke sternly to her or spanked her, she ultimately felt safe and protected—and aroused. Her talk with Sarah had helped her think through this dilemma somewhat, but she was still hung up on giving him permission to spank her. Could she do that? She was still playing this obstacle over and over in her head in a loop on Thursday night when Sarah called.

"Hey, how was your day with the munchkins?" Sarah asked cheerfully.

"Oh, it was fine," Lydia said without much expression.

"You sound a little down. Do you want to meet and talk? You could come over here if you like. Besides, I'd love to tell you about my day with Connor. God, Lydia, there is something about these McCauley boys!"

Lydia smiled and decided it would be a good idea and agreed to bring a bottle of wine and meet Sarah at her apartment in an hour.

Sarah began a sort of nonstop stream of consciousness about Connor from the time Lydia walked in the door, and after a couple of glasses of wine, she was revealing how she lusted after him and was dying for him to take her out.

Lydia smiled and said, "I'm happy for you, Sarah, and I hope things work out. But be warned that the McCauley brothers probably also share their idea that spanking is the preferred method for ending a disagreement or getting a message across about your health and safety."

"Yeah. I get that. I have to say, while Connor and I are not that close—yet—he has made veiled references about putting me across his knee and making it uncomfortable for me to sit for a few days if I did such and such. I think it's just part of who they are."

"But that's my problem," Lydia almost wailed. "I just can't give Cade permission to spank me, even if the aftereffects turn me on a little. What would I say? Sure, it's fine; go ahead and spank me?'"

"I don't think that's how it works, Lydia," Sarah said thoughtfully. "I think it's more like you submitting to a spanking without deciding to leave him because of it. No one likes getting her bare bottom scorched, and it's not like it would be a regular thing. I think you need to figure out if you can let that be part of your relationship without ending things. Does that make sense?"

Lydia thought about it and, yes, it did make sense. She didn't have to agree to be spanked. She just needed to agree not to call things off if it happened. That was something she thought she could live with.

Lydia threw her arms around Sarah. "You are the best friend ever, Sarah. This makes so much sense. And now I think Cade and I can pick up where we left off. I am so dying to be with him again!"

"I'm glad. What are you going to do?"

"Well, I can't just call him and say everything is fine if you spank me. I'm going to have to wait for him to call me so we can talk. I sure hope he calls this weekend. Oh, I feel like the weight of the world has been lifted off me, Sarah. Thank you."

As luck would have it, Lydia was to see Cade quite soon. On Friday, while she was teaching all day, she had left the back door of her old VW Bug ajar. The battery had drained so that by the time a coworker noticed it at lunch, it was dead. Sarah was the only person she knew who could jump a battery so she called her.

"Let me see if I can get away for a little while to come over there. The school is only about six blocks away from the site, right? I'll come when I can." Sarah was so helpful and calm about everything. Lydia went back to work and forgot about the car.

About 2:30 in the afternoon, Lydia was in the three-year-old classroom, singing, "You are my sunshine!" Most of the young students knew some signs but she was teaching the one for sunshine and laughing with them as they practiced. As she sang the last line, "Never take my sunshine away," she picked up one of the little girls and twirled her around. As she spun around, she stopped short as she saw Cade in the doorway watching her.

Cade's body completely filled the schoolroom doorway and Lydia gasped with surprise while she gently put the little girl down. Cade motioned her over with his finger. As Lydia made her way across the room, she noticed that everyone working in the area had stopped to watch. She blushed as she raced over, craned her neck up to look at him, and whispered loudly, "Cade! What are you doing here?"

"I just came to see my sunshine," he said in his gravelly voice that everyone could hear.

She blushed even deeper. "No, really! What—"

He interrupted her and said, "Sarah said you needed someone to come over to help you get your car going. I told her I would do it." He held out her car keys. "Here. I've got the battery charged, so you are good to go." Then he lowered his chin and raised his eyebrows. "So, you left the door open and the keys in the car? Do you do that often?"

She grabbed the keys, embarrassed to be watched by everyone. "No, well, not all the time," she answered tentatively.

"Let's add that to the list of things we are going to talk about tonight."

"What? Tonight? What's tonight?" Lydia asked, still trying to whisper.

"This is the night we are going to work things out once and for all," Cade said in a no-nonsense tone. "I want you to go home after school and I'll pick you up at 5:00."

"But where are we going? What are we doing?" Lydia questioned.

"Just let me handle everything," Cade said as he turned to walk down the hall. Then he turned back and called out, "Be ready at 5:00, sunshine!"

Lydia was so embarrassed, she briefly covered her face with her hands as she went back into the classroom with the children.

One of the students asked an assistant, "Did that man call Ms. Lang his sunshine?"

She chuckled and said, "I think so, Joey. I think so.

# Chapter 13

Cade texted Lydia at 4:30, to make sure she would be ready, and suggested they go for a fish fry at a local tavern. She loved the idea and went to dress appropriately. The October weather was making for chilly nights so she wore tights under a short denim skirt. The gray/green sweater she chose highlighted her already stunning green eyes and was form fitting enough to show off her trim midriff and perfectly proportioned breasts. It also had a deep V cut, making her feel sexy. She had just finished running a brush through her lustrous black mane when the doorbell rang. She ran to the door still stocking-footed and threw it open. She greeted Cade with a big smile as he looked her up and down.

He thought she looked amazing but was immediately struck with a possessiveness that told him didn't want any other man seeing her short skirt and tight, low-cut sweater. "You look great, Lydia," he said as he stepped in and shut the door.

"You too. I'm so glad to see you! I'll be ready in a second. Just let me get some boots," she said as she started back down the hall.

"Wait a minute, Lydia. Come back here," he said, more sternly than he had meant to. She looked up at him questioningly.

"You do look great, but that outfit is, well, it's something I'd rather you wear when we stay home."

Lydia was surprised as she looked down at what she had on. "You don't like it?"

"I like it—a lot. But so will any man who sees you in that short skirt and sweater that leaves nothing to the imagination."

There was a long pause as Lydia processed what he said. She was considering whether to fight this battle. "Do you want me to change my clothes?" she asked, a little incredulously.

"I would be more comfortable if you did," he said as he looked her in the eye.

Lydia decided this argument was best left for another day. She was so happy to be with him again after all. "Just give me a couple of minutes."

She changed into a loose, soft white tunic sweater, leggings and some high gray boots. When Cade saw her, he breathed a sigh of relief and said, "That white really shows off the color of your hair. Amazing!"

She smiled but said nothing.

He held her coat for her and turned her to face him. Then he pulled her forward to kiss her forehead and said, "Thank you."

Lydia pecked him on the cheek and said, "You're welcome. Let's go. I'm starving!"

The bar was crowded, but Cade knew the bartender, who signaled them to a corner booth that had just come up. After ordering a couple of beers and digging into a traditional perch dinner, he said, "I wanted to tell you how much I enjoyed seeing you at work in a different setting today. Those kids seemed to really love you. I think you're really good at what you do."

"That's kind of you to say," Lydia said with a little blush. "But I love those kids too. Next to working on site with you, it's my favorite assignment."

"Speaking of working on site, are you ready to come back next week? If I have to watch Connor and Sarah flirt for one more day..." he said as he rolled his eyes.

"Yes. I'm looking forward to coming back. I think we have that part of "us" worked out." When he looked at her with a question, she added, "I mean, I think we can work together and still maintain professionalism."

"I'm glad you're comfortable with that. The question remains then, if you can be comfortable with the idea of me spanking you when I feel you are not paying adequate attention to your health and safety."

Lydia gasped and choked a little on her coleslaw. After a few sips of water, she looked around to see if anyone had heard what Cade said, "Cade!" she said with an exaggerated whisper. "Please! We can't talk about that here." Her eyes held tears from choking and she now sported a full-blown red blush. She could not believe he brought up such a sensitive subject so casually—and so publicly. She was a little miffed so she became quiet and only picked at the rest of her food.

Cade understood that he had overstepped so he reached across the table to cover her hand with his and said, "I'm sorry, baby. I should have left that topic for a time when we could be private. Forgive me?"

"Okay," she said, but she was not really feeling okay. She had lost her appetite.

Finally, Cade asked, "Are you finished? We can go home and have some ice cream at my house if you want."

"I guess I'm ready to go," she huffed and began to slide out of the booth. But Cade was already standing and he blocked her way. He put one hand on the booth bench behind her and one on the table, leaned in, and talked so only she could hear.

"Listen, baby, I will not put up with any pouting or sass tonight. We have some important things to talk about and I want to talk to the grown-up Lydia. Am I clear?"

She looked way up at him and remembered to use words. "Yes, Cade," she said quietly.

"Good girl," he said as he helped her on with her coat, took her hand, and led her out through the crowded tavern.

Lydia was very quiet on the way home as she tried to think back on the things Sarah had told her about how to move forward.

After turning on the fireplace and settling in, Cade got them both a dish of mint chocolate ice cream and they ate in silence, each waiting for the other to begin. Finally, Lydia said, "I've been doing a lot of thinking about us… and about your needs."

"Yeah? What do you think my needs are?" he asked in a light tone.

"Well, you told me that you need to be the one in charge and you need to keep me safe."

"That's true."

"And you also said that if I don't, or if you think I've, oh, that if you are unhappy with my behavior, you will spank me," she said very fast.

"Also, true."

When Lydia paused, Cade said, "And so, you have been thinking about this?" He took her empty bowl from her and pulled her onto his lap, thinking it might be easier for her to talk if she didn't have to look him in the face yet felt secure in his arms. "I'd like to know what you decided."

Lydia took a deep breath. "Okay. Here's what I know. I know you spank me because you want me to be safe. And you also believe respect is very important so you will not have profanity."

She paused then, so he said, "You seem to understand me pretty well."

"I also know I hate your spankings. They hurt more than I think you imagine and they're humiliating. But I also know that besides a sore bottom, you would never hurt me—not really."

"Again, true," Cade said seriously.

She looked up at him then and said, "So, here's what I think. I think that while I cannot tell you it's okay to spank me, I won't end our relationship if you decide to do it."

When he began to answer, she said quickly, "Besides, I think I can be so good, you won't ever think you have to spank me."

Cade laughed out loud then. "Oh, baby, don't count on that! I've only known you for about a week and you've gotten a spanking, some warning swats, and narrowly missed at least one more."

Lydia folded her arms across her chest and said, "Well, how often do you think you will *have* to spank me?"

"I don't know, baby. You're going to have to try to behave and take your chances." And with that, he leaned in, grabbed her for a kiss, and moved his hands under her sweater to push her bra out of the way.

---

It was time to take this to the next level.

Lydia moaned into his mouth, relishing the feel of his calloused hands on her breasts. Then he reached down, pulled her sweater off and unclasped her bra. She was sitting before him naked from the waist up. Cade thought he had never seen more tantalizing breasts. They were just large enough to be a handful and those dusky nipples against her fair skin were amazing. His mouth moved to latch on to one of her nipples as he watched them become hard pebbles.

As Lydia began to writhe and whimper, Cade realized he needed to know some things before they went any further. So, he took her hands away from the back of his head and said, "Wait, baby, there are some things I need to know before we continue."

Lydia felt frustrated, though she wasn't sure why. She'd had very little sexual experience and truthfully didn't understand the longings she was feeling, but she knew she wanted to be as close to Cade as she could possibly be. Kissing was not at all enough. She did not know any "right" way to approach him so she decided to just follow her instincts. Lydia reached up, put her arms around Cade's neck, and with her lips touching his, said, "Cade, I need you. Haven't we talked enough?"

He could feel her warm little body pressed against his and when she whispered her need against his lips, he felt a jolt of lust. He began to think about how she would look and feel naked, open and under him. The thought was so powerful—and dangerous—that he had to pull away and shake his head. He actually took her arms and set her away from him. She looked confused and hurt. He had to talk fast.

"Baby, baby, listen." He kissed her forehead and again pulled back to meet her eyes. "I feel it too. Like I said, we have a strong connection, but we really need to take it slow." When she didn't respond, he continued, "I need to know some things about you."

"Like what? I thought you said you feel like you already know me," she asked impatiently.

"Well, yes, but I don't know some important details. For

example, how many boyfriends have you had? Are you on birth control? What do you like sexually?"

Lydia was a little stunned. What would he think when he found out how completely inexperienced she was? Would he laugh at her, or worse, decide she wasn't worth it? She felt tears of mortification prick at her eyes.

Again, he pulled her in for an embrace, saying, "Oh, Lydia, you can tell me the truth."

She had no choice but to be honest so she steeled herself for his reaction and then replied, "Okay. One. Yes. And I don't know."

Now it was Cade's turned to be stunned. "One boyfriend? I would think boys—and men—would be after you all the time. You're so beautiful!"

Lydia smiled sweetly and said, "Thank you, but I was always with my sister. I mean, I wouldn't do anything without her. The last few months are the first time my life has been separate from her. We were a package deal and no guys wanted that."

Cade counted his blessings, realizing that their meeting at this time of her life was pure luck. "Okay," he said, "but you're still on birth control?"

"Women take birth control for lots of reasons, Cade," she said with a little eye roll. "I've had trouble with my periods since I could remember, so my doctor suggested them a few years ago. It helps."

"I get it," he said. "But you know what? You're going to "get it" if I see another eye roll. That is a sign of disrespect that I won't tolerate."

"Sorry," she said as she lowered her eyes. She did not want to make him angry right now.

"And so, you slept with this 'one' boyfriend? What kinds of things do you like sexually?"

"Oh, Cade, I can't talk about it!"

He looked at her and waited.

Exasperated and embarrassed, she looked down and said, "There's not much to say. Yes, we slept together, slept being the operative word. It was after a homecoming dance. He gave me some beers—another thing I had never done—and then I remember him trying to take my clothes off and pawing at me and yelling at me. He tried to penetrate me but I, well, I just struggled hard to get away and I was sort of dizzy and drunk so I don't really know what happened. When he was done, I guess, he was really mad and he slapped me hard, told me to get dressed and took me home. That's it." She still couldn't look up at him, and she felt a big tear drip down her cheek.

"Goddammit, Lydia!" he said as stood up and began pacing. "What an asshole! What's this guy's name?"

"Cade, it was so long ago. We never dated after that and then he went off to the military. He's gone, Cade."

Cade reached for her and held her a little too tightly. "I can't believe that has been the extent of your sexual experience. Sex can be a beautiful thing. I hope I can show you what it's supposed to be like."

She looked up through tears and said, "So, you still want me? Even though I've never… I mean I don't know… I'm a virgin?"

The enormity of that statement was not lost on Cade. She was a virgin! It blew him away. He had never been with a woman as innocent and naive as Lydia. It was a big responsibility.

Lydia took his silence as disgust and pulled away from him. "Oh, Cade, I'm so sorry!" she said as she began to cry.

"Oh, sweet baby!" he said as he rocked her in his arms. "Don't be sorry. It's wonderful! You're going to be so much fun. I feel like I've won the lottery."

"Really?" She raised her tear-stained face to his. Then, shyly, she continued, "Can you show me now?"

Cade had never been so hard, but he had to consider her inexperience. "Do you really want this, Lydia?"

"I've never wanted anything more. Please. I feel, well, I feel, I don't know this feeling, but I know I need you. Please, Cade, take me to your bed."

That did it. He swooped her up and carried her down the hall to his bedroom. When they got to the end of the long hallway, he entered a huge room. Still holding her, he did not turn on a light but rather switched on a long gas fireplace whose flames gently lit up the incredible room. Besides the fireplace, there was a sitting area with a large screen television, huge windows overlooking a wooded yard, and the largest bed Lydia had ever seen.

"Oh my God, Cade, this bed is so huge," she said as he sat down and pulled her to stand between his legs.

"I had it custom made. Most beds are not tall enough for me so I gave them some specifics, and this is what they came up with."

Lydia had to admit that the height and expanse of the bed was a little intimidating. She was a little anxious, and he saw her look around for the en-suite.

"Oh, everything you need is in there," he said as he motioned toward the bathroom that turned out to be as big as the bedroom in Lydia's apartment. She excused herself and went to use the bathroom. It was beautifully appointed, with all the newest of fixtures and the fluffiest of towels. Yet the room, like his entire house, exuded a strong masculinity that Lydia found intoxicating. She must have taken too long because she heard him call, "Lydia, are you okay in there?"

"Oh, y-yes," she stammered, "I'll be right out."

Suddenly, Lydia had an idea. She knew Cade was wary of coming on too strong with her but she knew she wanted him to make love to her. Maybe she should make the first move. What would he do if she removed all of her clothes to reenter the bedroom naked? She was sure there would be no turning back after that. Quickly, she took off everything but her bra and panties, and then, deciding she might as well go for it, she removed those too.

Now Cade was at the door, "Lydia? Come on out, baby."

Completely naked now, she took a deep breath and opened the door. Cade was right there and she thought she would never forget the look of surprise—and desire—on his face at that moment for as long as she lived.

## Chapter 14

Cade was shocked into a momentary paralysis. Lydia stood in the doorway, framed by the soft light behind her. Her perfect breasts peeked out from the cascade of hair that hung almost to her hips. Her narrow waist flared out to shapely hips and trim legs. The tiny pink toes and her amazingly small feet finished off what Cade thought to be the most exquisite thing he had ever seen. All he could say was, "God, Lydia, you are absolutely gorgeous."

She threw her arms around his neck and pressed her naked body against his fully clothed one. She didn't know too much about sex but was sure she could feel his cock getting hard against her. Cade groaned and reached down to her bottom. He lifted her up and she put her legs around his waist. Lydia could have stayed just like that forever, but Cade had other ideas. He walked with her over to the bed, pulled down the covers, placed her down gently and crawled in next to her, wrapping her in his arms and putting one leg possessively over hers. Lydia tried to snuggle into his neck but he put his hand in her hair and moved her face to kiss her deeply and with purpose. Lydia tried to emulate the kiss, meeting his lips and tongue. She must have been doing it right because Cade swore and sat up to remove his clothes.

She watched as she saw Cade's body for the first time. She knew his shoulders were broad, but that muscular chest moving down to a tight waist and butt had Lydia actually whimpering.

Cade smiled at her. "Like what you see, baby?" he teased as he removed his pants.

When Lydia got a look at his cock, now fully erect and very large, she gasped. That couldn't possible fit inside her. She brought her hand up to her mouth, wondering how she was going to get out of this now.

"Don't worry, baby, we'll take it slow. Tonight, everything is about you."

Lydia didn't know what that meant but it comforted her.

Cade moved his head down to suckle at her breasts, and when he gave one a gentle bite, she arched up to meet his mouth with a little cry. She grabbed at his head to keep him there but he said, "Relax, Lydia, and let me do the work. Just go with it if you can."

Breathlessly, Lydia said, "Oh, Cade, I don't know... I never felt... I just don't know how to do this."

"It's all good, baby, just try to relax," he said as he moved his hand down to her mons to cup her there. When he gently put a finger inside her to find her clit, she felt a jolt of desire and naturally spread her legs.

Cade smiled.

"Oh, Cade, what are you doing to me?"

"I'm taking you for a ride, little girl. Just follow my lead."

As he stroked her clit and inserted another finger, he paid close attention to her reaction. He was delighted. She was a sensual woman just coming to understand herself, and he was the one to teach her. His cock sprang to life.

Lydia was just about frantic with desire as he stroked her clit and bit at her breasts. She moaned, arched her back, and moved with such raw reaction that Cade didn't know how long he could hold out. But when she moved her hands to his head and pulled at his hair, he stopped her. "Lydia, if you pull my hair again, I'll stop, turn you over and spank you until you understand. Put your hands above your head."

*Oh my god.* She was knew he didn't know how those stern words upped her intensity but she put her hands above her head. He grabbed her wrists together and kept them there while his other hand drove her mad. The feelings were so strong and raw and new for her that she was a little frightened.

"Cade, stop! Stop! I think I'm going to faint. I don't know this feeling."

"I know, baby. Try to relax and let it happen. You're almost there."

And indeed, as he stroked her clit and the rough spot near it, she felt herself ascend as if into space. And then she was there, moving in tandem with his hand and screaming in pleasure. Her body had a sheen that came from exertion and she was breathing hard and rapidly. She felt out of control as she hit the pinnacle. She actually saw stars. Her sense of euphoria retreated slowly and deliciously. Cade held her as she came down, kissing her face gently and murmuring encouragement. A smile of supreme contentment came over Lydia's face that made Cade think he was the luckiest man in the world. But he could no longer wait. He moved to cover her body while supporting himself with his elbows.

Her eyes were closed so he said, "Lydia, open your eyes, I want to see your face when I make love to you." Her eyes sprang open and he could see conflicting emotions of trepidation and desire. "I love you, Lydia, but I think this is going to hurt a little at first. I want you to be brave and see it through. I believe it will be worth it. Are you ready?"

Lydia bit her lip but nodded.

Cade guided his cock to her entrance. She was wet and ready for him so he moved in slowly. My god, she was tight, but he knew if he was patient, she would adjust to accommodate him. He watched her face for signs she was in pain, but instead, he saw her working hard to please him.

"Are you okay, baby?" he asked, concerned.

"Oh, Cade, I want you inside me. Please!"

With that, Cade moved into her and on the second thrust, he felt her barrier give way as she cried out. He kept moving slowly, all the while watching her face as the look of pain disappeared and lust took over.

"I'm fine, Cade. More than fine. This is wonderful!" she said breathlessly.

So, Cade picked up his rhythm and they moved together until he lost control and came powerfully inside her. They cried out together, then he slowed his pace until their breathing became more even. He was still impaled inside her and she was still squirming. Cade thought this was as close to heaven as he could get.

Finally, he pulled out slowly and lay next to her, pushing the wet strands of her hair off her face and kissing her eyelids. "You are magnificent, Lydia Lang."

"Mm, you too," she replied as she cuddled in close to him and fell asleep.

Cade watched the satisfied smile on her face and her breathing becoming easy and rhythmic. God, he loved this girl!

He got a warm washcloth and gently washed between her legs. He was reminded then that she had been a virgin and he was moved to tears by that responsibility. His protective nature overcame him as he lay down next to her, put a leg possessively over her body and brought the sheets over them.

They made love two more times that night and several times the next day. Cade was amazed and thrilled at how insatiably sensuous his girl turned out to be. That, combined with enough of a submissive nature to perfectly complement his dominance, made her the perfect woman for him.

## Chapter 15

I t had been difficult for Lydia to leave Cade's bed and go
home after a weekend of lovemaking, but she was also
looking forward to beginning their time together on the
work site. So, on Monday when Lydia awoke in her own bed,
she at first felt bereft because Cade's big warm body was not
there for her to snuggle. But when she thought about the life-
changing weekend she had spent with him learning the
delights of sex, she got tingly all over. She was in love and it
was amazing!

The day dawned sunny and warm for October in Wisconsin, and Lydia was up with the birds. She was so excited to go
back to the work of helping hearing-impaired high school
students transition into the workplace. Now that Cade had
talked through the path of their relationship and she was
finally coming to know herself, she was ready to get back to
work at the building site where she would be with Cade all
day. She was beginning to develop a sense of herself outside
of her relationship with her sister and she could feel a sense of
confidence building.

Today, the project began in earnest, with the students

being added to the schedule at the construction site. The goal was to allow them to work in as close to a normal routine and environment as possible. Lydia, whose job was to translate directions and questions, was the key to making that happen. She felt confident about her ASL skills as well as her background in construction.

After picking up the students in the school van and getting them to the site, Lydia arrived and led them to the group meeting just as Cade was beginning to give directions for the day. His looks made her heart skip a beat, just as they had when she first saw him a couple of weeks ago. His angular face was covered in a stubble of beard and his work clothes could not disguise his muscular physique. As he was about 6'3", he stood out above most of the other workers and as he gave the orders for the day in his deep, rumbly voice, he exuded leadership and the dominance that Lydia now knew that she loved. Suddenly, she heard him say her name as he talked to his crew, and she was dragged out of her reverie.

"This, as many of you know, is Ms. Lydia Lang who is the ASL interpreter for the students who will be with us for at least the next two months. She will help with any communication between you and the students. Our goal is help these students transition into a real-life work experience. Your cooperation will be much appreciated. Ms. Lang, do you have anything you would like to say?"

She was caught off guard but did not want to pass on the opportunity to introduce her students and herself. After realizing that her voice did not carry like Cade's, they found her a bullhorn and she briefly explained her role and made introductions. She stole a glance at Cade, who did not meet her eyes but explained to the group that Connor would be directly supervising her group and should be consulted with any questions or concerns.

While he spoke, Lydia was able to look around at Cade's

crew. In general, they seemed like regular guys, and while she understood this was new for them, she hoped they were all as friendly as they looked. That is except for a couple of younger guys off to the side. She saw that they had been rudely ignoring Cade, talking to each other, and seemed to be snickering at her students. She had experienced this kind of biased treatment many times in life with her sister and also with students at school. She hoped these guys would not be trouble.

Connor had divided her students into three workgroups stationed close enough together to make supervising them easier, and the morning went very smoothly. As the workers got familiar with the students and watched her "speak" with them, they became more comfortable with talking slowly and face to face, so lip reading could happen, and even picked up some signs. Connor checked in a few times but Cade kept his distance. Lydia found herself disappointed even though she understood they had to maintain professional space.

The minute Cade laid eyes on Lydia that morning, he knew that working together while not acknowledging a relationship was going to be harder than he thought. First of all, even dressed in overalls and work boots, Lydia was beautiful. That incredible mop of black hair gathered in a knot on her head, her fair skin contrasting with her cheeks which had been made rosy with the cool day, her brilliant smile, and the silvery sound of her voice as she spoke and laughed with her students, made him want to whisk her off somewhere private, divest her of her clothes and have his way with her. The memory of her naked, aroused, perfect body and that adorable little bottom was distracting. That he could not even pay her much attention on site, especially when most of the other workers were knocking themselves out to get noticed by her, just about drove him crazy. However, he had to meet the challenge of working together as they had agreed.

At lunch, a few of the students felt comfortable enough to

eat with their work groups but Angie, the only girl, looked a little lost. Lydia noticed and signed for her to sit and eat with her. As Lydia unpacked her lunch, she noticed that Angie didn't have one. She had been so anxious that morning, she had forgotten her lunch. Lydia immediately gave Angie the sandwich and cookie she had brought. There was a cooler with water for the workers so Lydia sent Angie to get a bottle.

Connor walked over and asked Lydia how things were going. He told her that he was happily surprised how well the kids fit in and that their skill level was actually above some apprentice workers he had seen. Just then, Angie came back with her water. She had been walking fast and when Lydia looked in her face, she saw there were tears. Connor took his leave and Lydia signed for Angie to walk with her. They walked to the edge of the site where Lydia could privately ask Angie what happened. Angie explained to Lydia that when she went over to the cooler, there were two guys who began calling her names and swearing at her. Angie was not entirely deaf so she could make out most of what they said. Lydia asked her to say exactly what they said and though she didn't want to repeat it, she did. They had called her a freak and talked about what they would like to do to her sexually. They said they could get away with it because she couldn't tell anyone. Lydia was enraged, but she had never handled anything like this before and knew she had to stay calm. She settled Angie down and asked if she wanted to leave. Angie said if she left, those jerks had won and she didn't want that. Lydia understood, but she was responsible for the safety and welfare of these students and could not let this stand. Lydia and Angie talked it over and decided to go to Cade.

When they found him, he could see they were upset. Their faces were pink and Angie had been crying. Lydia looked angry. He led them to the site trailer to talk. It was a very uncomfortable report as the guys had used vulgar language when calling her names and described explicit sex acts as they thought she couldn't hear. Lydia had never translated some of the words before and she was embarrassed and increasingly angry. Cade was furious!

"Goddammit! Who were the guys? Show me. They're gone today! Goddammit!" he yelled and as he stood, he knocked his chair over. Cade, this angry, was a sight to behold. Lydia mentally noted that she would want to avoid this at all costs in the future. The sound startled Angie and tears escaped down her cheeks.

Lydia put an arm around her and said, "Please, Cade. Wait. Can we ask Angie what she thinks is appropriate?"

"I'll listen to her, but these are my workers, on my site, Lydia, and in the end, I say what goes."

"I understand, Cade," she said in a placating tone.

Angie went outside with Cade and identified the two men who had harassed her.

Cade called them in. They were brothers—Daryl and David Caruthers. They were young and rough around the edges, but Cade had decided to give them a chance when he hired them. He was angry and moved toward then. Lydia quickly stood up between them, hoping to prevent any physical altercation.

Cade grabbed her and put her behind him as if to shield her. Almost growling, he said, "You stay there, I'll handle this." Cade told them what Angie had heard them say and their faces went white.

"Christ, Mr. McCauley, we thought she was deaf. We didn't know she could hear us."

Again, Cade moved toward them, causing the young men to step back.

Lydia grabbed at the back of his jacket.

Cade was yelling now. "What the hell difference does that make? You said it! We don't hold with that kind of language here, never mind that no man of any worth *ever* talks to a woman like that. You're fired! Both of you! Get out!"

"But, Mr. McCauley, give us another chance."

"I gave you a chance. There is no excuse for treating anyone, much less those more vulnerable, in such a disgusting manner. You have shown your character. You are not the kind of men I can employ. Turn in your gear and get off the site. I'll have HR send out the paperwork."

Daryl leveled a look on Cade, and then on Lydia, and said, "You haven't heard the last from us, asshole."

Suddenly, Cade had the man by the scruff of his neck, picked him up off the floor and threw him out the door. His brother scrambled after him.

"Don't you dare threaten me or anyone on my site? One more word, and I'll get the police involved. Do I need to take you to your cars?"

The Caruthers brothers turned and stomped off, muttering profanities.

Cade stood watching them with his hands held into fists. When he turned back to the girls, he saw Lydia hunkered down in front of Angie, holding her hands and speaking in a gentle, comforting voice. He was reminded again what a compassionate and competent woman Lydia was.

She turned to Cade and said, "Can we talk alone here for a little while? We need to determine our next steps."

Cade sighed and pulled up a folding chair next to Angie so he could look her in the eye. "Angie, I am so sorry this happened to you today. I don't know if you want to leave or if you ever want to come back, but I hope you will. Those men are gone now and no one will ever bother you again on this site. Do you understand?"

Angie nodded and said bravely, "Thank you, Mr. McCauley. I'll be okay."

Cade stood and made his way to the trailer door. He

looked at Lydia and said, "Let me know if you need my help. I'll be close by."

The next couple of hours were stressful for Angie and Lydia. Angie had decided she wanted to stay, but Lydia had to call her supervisor to let him know what had transpired. He was calm and helpful but said that they would need to meet at the end of the day to make sure everything was handled appropriately.

As they finished up and got ready to leave, Lydia approached Cade. "My supervisor called and asked if I could attend a meeting this afternoon. Apparently, Angie's parents will be there. I told him I would be there as soon as I dropped off the other students."

Cade surprised Lydia by saying, "Yeah, he called me too and asked if I would come to the meeting. I told him I thought that was appropriate. So, I'll be there with you. Do you want to ride with me?"

Lydia groaned but then straightened her shoulders and said, "No, you know I have to drive the kids back in the van. I'll meet you there."

As it turned out, the meeting went as well as it could have. Angie's parents were teachers themselves. They were concerned but satisfied that their daughter would be safe continuing with the project. Cade's apology and promise had gone a long way in setting the tone for the meeting. Lydia was asked to write up a report on the incident but assured them that it would not become public. Lydia, though, still upset, felt much better as they walked out of school.

Cade walked the quiet Lydia to her car and said, "Hey, this was a long, hard day for you. Why don't you let me pick up food and bring it over to your house?"

"I don't think I'll be very good company tonight," she said tiredly.

"You don't have to be. I just want to be sure you eat and get settled in. What do you feel like eating?"

She looked up at him appreciatively. "I feel like Chinese. Is that okay with you?"

An hour later, they were eating dinner at her kitchen island. Lydia thought back on the meeting with Angie's parents that could have been so unpleasant. She looked up at Cade and said, "You know, I don't think I told you how much I appreciated the way you handled the parent meeting today. You didn't even have to be there, but your kind professionalism went a long way to diffusing the situation. Thank you."

"I'm glad things worked out. I was pretty impressed with you too, baby. I think we make a good team," he said as he picked up their plates and began to clean up. She stood, and he came to put his hands on her hips. "Listen, I know you're tired. I'm going to clean up here while you take a shower and get into your pajamas. Then you are going to bed."

"No! No, I have to write that report—"

Cade stopped her and said, "I heard what your boss said. That report doesn't need to be in until Friday. Tonight, you need to rest."

Lydia stomped her foot like an angry child and opened her mouth to argue.

Cade put his hand behind her head and kissed her, thus stifling her protests. When he finally pulled away, he said, "I am not going to argue with you. You are getting ready for bed. If you'd like a spanking first, I can arrange that. Am I clear?"

She gave him a defiant look, but he turned her in the direction of the bedroom, applied a substantial smack to her bottom, and said, "Do as I say. Now."

Even after her stressful day, his words had an arousing effect on her. Her panties got a little damp every time he took charge. But she was too tired to think that dilemma through tonight. She took a quick shower and just as she finished slipping into her most comfortable PJs, Cade was in her room saying, "You're tired tonight, but we are going to have to talk about the threats the Caruthers brothers made. I think we are going to install more security cameras around the site and I wouldn't mind if you had one here at home, too. There may be some safety rules I am going to ask you to follow."

"Oh, Cade, I know how to be safe. Please don't make me live with a bunch of rules," Lydia whined and then yawned.

"Like I said, tonight is not the night, but we will be addressing this tomorrow," Cade said as he put his finger on her lips to silence her complaints. "Let's get you tucked in, baby." He pulled the covers up over her and actually tucked them tightly under the mattress.

Lydia looked at him, surprised. She thought he might get in bed with her. "You mean you're not going to... well, you're not going to... to stay?"

He chuckled and tapped her nose like a child. "I'll lock up on my way out," and then a little more gruffly, "sleep, now."

But it was a long while before Lydia actually slept.

## Chapter 16

After that dramatic start to the week, Lydia was anxious to get into a routine with Cade and also at work. The October weather was perfect for doing the outside work on the build site and they were making progress with the house. The students had fallen into a comfortable routine and Cade's workers were doing a great job with them. She even saw some of the crew signing to her students who were hearing-impaired. She appreciated their kindness and effort.

Truthfully, the most difficult part of the job had turned out to be the agreement she had made with Cade to keep everything professional and show no signs of their relationship while at work. Just being around Cade, sometimes made Lydia vibrate with desire. She had to concentrate to keep her mind off him.

Cade felt much the same. Being so close to her all day but maintaining a distance was difficult. Not only did he want to be with her, but he also worried when she was using power tools or climbing on ladders. Added to that, was the fact that Lydia's personality and beauty did not go unnoticed by the other workers. Many times during the day, he would see one of the guys talking or laughing with Lydia. He had to admit he was unreasonably jealous so it was yet another thing to deal with.

They were together almost every night, usually at his place that was a little more remote than her house, and that helped them keep their relationship on the down low. They discovered that they had many tastes and opinions in common, though Cade was more conservative, and could easily watch movies that the other had chosen and talk about current events.

And the sex—it was explosive! Cade delighted in teaching Lydia the intense pleasure that could be had in bed. Privately, he reveled in the fact that her inexperience and submissive tendencies allowed him to call the shots and dominate her in the bedroom, and more importantly, she seemed to like it. He had noticed after the times he had spanked her, that though she protested energetically, she was more ready for him than ever. After he introduced her to "play" spankings, he thought she was probably anal erotic. But he would take that slowly.

For her part, Lydia was shocked to find making love so thrilling. She had no idea there were so many ways to produce an orgasm, and he often brought her to multiple ones on any given night. She was still a little embarrassed that she loved it so much, including his dominance, which she seemed to like in and out of the bedroom. She still didn't understand it. The times that Cade had spanked her for real were very painful and she fought to get away. But later, as he held her on his lap with her bare bottom bright red and throbbing, she was inevitably consumed by an overwhelming feeling of safety and comfort. She began to believe he cared for her very much though her frequent disbelief that a man like him would fall for a young, inexperienced woman like her still rustled up feelings of insecurity.

They had shared their situation with almost no one. Cade's brother Connor and Lydia's sister Lola, who was far away at school, knew about it as well as Lydia's best friend Sarah. The construction crew was also surely aware of their relationship but they respected Cade and did not tease or talk about it. Lydia knew they had to maintain the ruse but she found herself wishing they could go out together once in a while or at least act more natural in public. However, this school-to-work project meant so much to her and she would not do anything to jeopardize its success. Cade knew how much that program mattered to her, so he was willing to do what it took.

About a week after Cade had fired the Caruthers brothers, he got a call from the company lawyer, Tom Desmond, informing him that the brothers had hired a lawyer and tried to bring a lawsuit against him for unlawful dismissal. Cade had talked to Tom about the incident so the lawyer had been able to counter the false claims being made and the suit was dropped. However, Tom had said, "Cade, there's not much risk of a lawsuit, but I met the brothers and they are tough, nasty guys. They are deep down angry about being fired and had no problem using threatening language right in front of me. Make sure you stay out of their way. Do you have security cameras at your sites?"

Security cameras were standard on most projects but not always on Home for Everyone sites. Cade thanked Tom for the information and set Connor to the task of installing cameras ASAP.

On Thursday night, Lydia decided to stay at her house and catch up on laundry and bills, etcetera. Cade had talked to her about moving in with him, but she was just not completely ready.

In the middle of the night, Lydia thought she heard some odd sounds coming from outside, near the garage. In the old neighborhood where she lived, garages were not only separate but often set at the back of the lots, so they were a distance from the house. Though she heard some strange sounds, they were not really loud and when she looked out the window, she couldn't see anything. Connor had said he was coming that weekend to install motion sensitive outdoor lights and some cameras, but for now it was pretty dark out there. She considered calling Cade but there was really nothing to report but some sounds that had now stopped.

As soon as Lydia opened her garage door the next morning, she understood what she must have heard. Her sweet little VW had been vandalized. There was glass and metal everywhere as well as spray-painted profanity in black, all over the outside and inside of the car. Lydia was so shocked that she couldn't immediately process what she saw. She stood there as silent tears coursed down her cheeks.

With trembling fingers, she grabbed her phone and called Cade who was already at the site. When he answered, she had trouble finding words. "Cade, my c-car... wrecked... b-broke into garage," she stammered breathlessly, making little sense.

Cade knew there was something very wrong, so he said, "Lydia, listen to me. I want you to go back into the house and wait for me. I'll be there in a minute. Do you hear me? Go back into the house and lock the door!"

Then he called Connor to meet him at Lydia's. When they pulled up, they saw Lydia sitting on her knees in the driveway near the open garage door. She seemed to be in shock. Cade leaped out of the truck and raced to her. He kneeled next to Lydia and looked at her tear-streaked face. He slowly and gently drew her onto his lap, rocking her and murmuring comfort.

Connor had gone to look at the car and now came back to Cade. He was furious and his face reflected the anger but to shield Lydia, he calmly said, "When you get a chance, Cade, you need so see this." Then he leaned into Cade's ear so only he could hear and said, "I called the police. They'll be here soon. Maybe get Lydia as settled as you can. They'll have questions for her."

Three hours later, the police were gone and some of Cade's crew was almost finished cleaning up what was left of the car in the garage. Connor had gone back to work and called Sarah to work with the students. Cade had helped Lydia get dressed in comfortable clothes and made sure she was staying hydrated. Some color had returned to her face and Cade was making her a sandwich that he hoped she could eat.

He brought her lunch out on a tray and set it on the ottoman in front of her. "I know you may not be hungry but I want you to eat a few bites—please," Cade said gently.

Lydia looked at his sincere face, then at the tray, and picked up the cookies and began to nibble.

"Can I just have the cookies?" she asked and he saw a small smile. She was coming back.

"You can have whatever you want, little girl." He leaned over and kissed her forehead. "Everything is going to be okay. The guys are almost finished cleaning up, the police think they have what they need to go after the Caruthers brothers, and today, you and I are going to load up what you need to move you to my house—for now," he added as her eyes flew to his face.

She surprised him by responding almost in a whisper, "Okay."

After they moved her things to his house in the afternoon, Cade insisted she take a nap. There were dark circles under her eyes and she was looking fragile. She put up a fuss until he turned her over his knee, pulled down her pants and panties, and said, "You're taking a nap, with or without a spanking. Which will it be?" When she didn't answer, he brought his hand down in a stinging slap that left his huge handprint covering her entire bottom. "Answer me, Lydia," he warned.

"Okay! I'll nap, you bully."

He replaced her clothes and tucked her in. Then he spent the day directing things by phone and getting some paperwork done. When Lydia woke up, she was feeling better but they spent the rest of the day and evening lounging on the sectional. Cade needed to have her safe in his arms, which is where she slept all night.

## Chapter 17

The next morning after they showered and ate, Lydia looked much better and had some of her spunk back. As they cleaned up, Cade tried to have a serious talk with her about the threats coming from the Carutherses. He told her that he didn't want her going *anywhere* alone until he thought the threat had lessened.

Lydia's response indicated that she was not appropriately worried when she said, "I am not going to check with you every time I go somewhere. What kind of life is that? I'm not a child! I took a self-defense class and I carry mace in my purse. I'm sure I'll be fine."

Cade could not believe how ridiculous that sounded. His concern for her safety and frustration at her casual attitude pushed his temper to its limit quickly. It was just yesterday that her car had been destroyed and those maniacs had been on her property. They could have easily broken into her house and—well, God knew what! Cade picked Lydia up and trapped her on the very familiar kitchen counter. He worked to keep himself from exploding in anger.

"Self-defense class! What? Do you remember what kind of

guys those brothers are? Do you remember what your car looked like? I am taking their threats seriously and so are you, Goddammit!"

Now she was angry. She lifted her chin and yelled back at him, "I swear, Cade, I will not be made a prisoner who has to check with her guard whenever I make a move. And you can't make me!"

Almost immediately, Lydia realized the mistake she had made. She had issued a challenge to him from which he would not back down. He lifted her off the counter and flung her over his shoulder. She screamed and beat at his back all the way to the bedroom where he was taking her. She knew where this was going but fought tooth and nail. It didn't even slow him down.

Cade sat down on the corner of his huge, high bed, flipped her over and yanked down her yoga pants and panties. His huge hands delivered searing swats to her bottom and thighs. He gave her twenty to thirty hard smacks before he began to lecture her. She was already crying, but he was still yelling so she heard every word.

"From now on, I need to know where you are at all times. You need to check with me," he said as he paused spanking for a moment but then started right back up. "This is not a negotiation!" he said as he actually sped up the smacks. "Do you understand?"

Lydia had never been in so much pain. He was truly setting her bottom on fire but she was mad too, so she recklessly screamed between sobs, "No! I will not! Cade, please stop. It hurts!!"

Lydia thought she actually heard him growl as he picked her up, threw her over his shoulder again, and made his way into the bathroom. He slammed through a couple of the drawers she used for her things, and apparently found what he was looking for. As he turned to go back into the bedroom,

Lydia caught sight of herself in the floor to ceiling bathroom mirror. She could see her bright red and mottled bottom and thighs obscenely slung over his shoulder and then, to her horror, she saw what he had found in the drawer—her hairbrush! She began to kick and squirm for all she was worth, but she was no match for Cade as he sat back down, plunked her over one of his tree trunk thighs and, as he secured her legs with his other one, began to paddle her, hard and fast. If Lydia had thought the spanking up to now hurt, she was completely unprepared for the intensity of being paddled with a hairbrush. The sting was ten times as bad. Her screaming was making her voice hoarse and she was having difficulty breathing between yelps.

Finally, after maybe twenty searing spanks, he stopped but still held the brush against her burning flesh. "So now, tell me. Are you ready to stay safe and check with me wherever you go? Think about your answer, little girl, because I will keep paddling until I know you agree."

Lydia could not face even one more spank, and as she took some deep breaths through her sobs, she said, "Yes! Yes, Cade. I'll do what you say. Please don't paddle me anymore!" She went limp then and her sobbing helped him feel she understood. He dropped the brush, grabbed some tissues near the bed, and turned her over onto his lap. She hissed as her bottom contacted his rock-hard thigh, but then he moved her so that her flaming butt balanced between his legs.

He wiped her face and then began to rock her, saying, "That's a good girl. I need you to listen to me. You understand what I am saying, right?"

With her forehead pressed into his neck, she nodded as her breathing became more even.

Cade stood up and carried her with him out to his recliner in the great room. He grabbed a soft throw, sat down, and covered both of them. He kept rocking gently as she let out an occasional sob and hiccup. Then her breathing changed and became even. She had fallen asleep. The quiet gave Cade time to think about his feelings for Lydia. The abject fear he felt when he thought about the Caruthers boys going after her, and the deep tenderness he felt holding his sweet, sleeping girl, made him realize that he wanted to be with Lydia for the rest of their lives. He wanted her in that bed every night. He wanted to marry her.

After he had laid her down on his bed—tummy side down —and tucked her in, he pushed some long locks off her face and placed a chaste kiss on her forehead. Did he feel any remorse about giving her the hardest spanking she had ever had? No. She had not been prepared to listen to him about her safety and he would do anything to protect her—even administer a long, hard spanking. He planned to keep an eagle eye on her until the Caruthers situation was resolved.

## Chapter 18

Lydia slept so deeply that she didn't even begin to wake until she saw sun peeking through the blinds in Cade's large bedroom and smelled coffee. She stretched and rolled onto her back, only to be given an immediate reminder of what had transpired the night before. Her bottom was still tender, so she rolled back to her tummy and reflected. She should be really angry with Cade. He was so high-handed and domineering. She did not want to have to check with him on her whereabouts all the time. But she did understand his position and even appreciated that he wanted to keep her safe. Still that spanking—and paddling—had been just awful and she wanted him to feel guilty about it. Maybe she could even seduce an apology out of him. Smiling to herself, she washed, brushed her hair, and even put on a little lip gloss. Then she grabbed the shirt he had been wearing the night before and put it on. It came to her mid thighs and she left the top several buttons open. Satisfied that she looked at least a little sexy, she padded out to the kitchen. She stopped in the doorway and waited for him to see her.

He gave her a big, beautiful smile when he saw her and said, "Morning, babe. Sit down, I'll get you some coffee."

"Thank you for the coffee, but I think I'll stand," she said with a pout as she moved to wrap her arms around him from the back and was so close that her breasts pressed up against his back.

Not planning on any apology, Cade replied, "Suit yourself. I'm making eggs, how would you like yours?"

Lydia mustered the best sulky tone she could and said, "I'm not hungry, thank you."

Cade put down the eggs and turned to stand in front of her, handing her a coffee cup. Lydia put down the mug and moved her hands to his chest, rubbing seductively and looking up at him with what she hoped was a sexy smile. Cade saw what the little minx was doing. He did not respond. Cade gently but firmly took her chin in his thumb and forefinger and raised her face to look at him. He was so close that she had to look way up to make eye contact.

"In this house, we eat breakfast. I'm going to ask you again. How do you want your eggs?"

When she didn't answer right away, he reached around, pulled her close, planted his giant hand on her tender bottom and said, "I expect an answer, little girl."

*So much for getting the upper hand,* she thought as she answered compliantly, "Scrambled hard, please, and thank you."

"Coming right up. And you will sit down. Now."

Lydia wished she had at least put her yoga pants back on to make it more comfortable to sit but she climbed up and sat down gingerly. She would feel that spanking for most of today, she thought with annoyance.

As if he could read her mind, he said, "I expect that naughty bottom to be tender for most of the day today. That's part of the spanking deal—something to help you remember that you need to check in with me wherever you go from now on."

When he turned back to the stove, Lydia muttered sassily under her breath, "Part of the spanking deal," and stuck her tongue out at him just as he turned to see that.

Now he slammed the pan down on the stove, and in a flash, he picked her up off the stool, turned her under his arm and re-lit the fire from the previous night with a dozen smacks to her still swollen butt. He didn't let her up but said instead, "That kind of sass makes me think you didn't understand that spanking last night. I am fine with starting all over again if it will cure you of that attitude. And another thing, don't you ever try that seductive act on me again. That will backfire every time. Do you understand?"

"Yes, yes!" she cried. "Please let me up. I'll be good. I promise. Please, Cade, I'm sorry!"

"Sit down while you still can, little girl."

She sat down once again, cowed by him.

While they ate, Cade decided to bring up a topic that might not sit well with Lydia. "Lydia, I've been thinking. It's not safe for you to stay at your house on your own right now. I'd like you to move in here with me—permanently."

"I don't know, Cade. I don't think we could keep the fact that we were living together a secret. What about keeping it professional, like we talked about?"

"Yeah, I understand, but your safety means more to me than any meaningless gossip. Please say you'll stay with me here, where I can keep you safe."

Truthfully, Lydia was frightened that he was right and it would be easier for the Caruthers brothers to carry out their threats if she was home alone. His concern for her safety won her over. If she was honest with herself, the idea of being near him all the time was a dream come true.

Cade spent the afternoon and early evening getting some

work done outside. He came in to find that Lydia had moved everything she brought with her into one of the smaller bedrooms.

He was not happy but she pleaded with him to allow her some of her own space. Finally, he said, "You can keep your things in the other bedroom, but you will be keeping your little body in my bed. Got it?"

Lydia smiled and said, "I got it, Cade."

## Chapter 19

Unfortunately, they found out that there was no way to prove it was the Caruthers brothers who had broken into her garage and damaged her car, so Cade's anxiety over her safety was always on high idle. Those guys were still out there.

Still, after a couple of weeks, Lydia and Cade fell into a comfortable routine. Their days were spent at work on the Home for Everyone site. His brother Connor was the direct supervisor for Lydia and her students, but Cade was around most of the time—sometimes being called away for meetings on future projects. Lydia felt her students were progressing with their skills really well, and by the time the weather turned quite cold, the work on the outside of the house would be nearly complete. Then they would get ready to work inside.

Connor, Sarah, and her sister Lola were the only people who knew about their living arrangement and Cade and Lydia could trust them. Connor's relationship with Sarah had progressed to the point that while they were not intense like Cade and Lydia, they were dating exclusively. It was really helpful to have such a good friend with whom to confide.

Every day, after work, Lydia drove the students back to school and then went "home" to Cade's house. This schedule allowed them to be discreet about their relationship and living arrangements.

Neither Cade nor Lydia had lived with anyone before, so it seemed likely there would be a period of adjustment. They both expected it and were happily surprised that there was very little conflict. Their division of labor worked out quite naturally, sharing cooking and cleaning responsibilities, with Cade doing the most outdoor work while Lydia did laundry and inside organizing. After a couple of weeks, Lydia had ended up going over Cade's knee for a spanking just once— but it had been memorable.

He had come home on a Saturday afternoon to find her outside, balancing on an extension ladder at the highest peak of the large two-story window at the front of the house. She had climbed up barefoot and was reaching precariously as high as she could. And she was alone. The idea of what could have happened to her raised his blood pressure and temper. When Lydia heard the truck pull in and saw Cade slam the door and come striding purposefully toward the ladder, it was the first time she had considered that he might not like her in this position.

Cade stood at the bottom of the ladder, holding it steady. How the hell had she managed to set up this huge piece of equipment by herself?

"What the hell are you doing? Get down here right now," Cade bellowed.

Lydia thought maybe she could explain things, so she made no move to come down but called out, "Somehow, birds made a really ugly mess up here and I wanted to wash it off before it got hard. I'm almost done."

"You're done now! Get down, or I will come up and get you and you will not be happy about that!"

Lydia already wasn't happy and because he was clearly quite mad, she figured she might as well quickly wash off the rest of the mess as long as she was up there.

When Cade saw her continue with her work instead of moving to come down, he exploded. "Goddammit, Lydia, did you hear what I said? All right, that's it." Cade began up the ladder and Lydia realized she had pushed him too far.

"No, wait! I'll come down now. Please just go back down. I'll be okay." Now she was worried.

Cade reached her, grabbed her tools and threw them to the ground, and put his arm around her waist like a steel band. "We'll do this together. Take a step."

After a couple of steps, Lydia got a cramp in her bare foot and couldn't help but yelp, "Oh, I have a cramp! It hurts!"

Cade reached down and gently massaged until the cramp subsided but then said angrily, "Never, never, go up a ladder barefoot! Goddammit, Lydia! Do you ever think?"

Tears pricked at her eyes as she said, "I'm sorry, Cade."

"Not as sorry as you're going to be, little girl! Keep stepping!"

When they reached the ground, Cade put her down and asked, "Can you stand?"

When she nodded, he turned her under his arm and applied at least twenty smacks to her jeans-covered bottom. When he let her up, he yelled, "I'm going to put away this ladder while you go into the bedroom and wait for me, standing with your nose in the corner. She looked at him pleadingly, but he said, "And pull down your pants and panties while you wait. Now go!" He gave her one more smack to send her on her way.

---

Cade watched as Lydia hurried inside, rubbing her bottom all the way. Would she do as he said? He really didn't know.

By the time he had stored the ladder and put everything away, he was calmer but still determined to teach his girl a lesson. There were so many dangerous and even deadly things that could have happened because she chose to climb that tall extension ladder alone—and barefoot! He never wanted her doing that or anything like it again. This called for a hard lesson.

Cade hung up his jacket, washing his hands and face off in the kitchen and then poured himself a shot of whiskey before heading to his bedroom. He really wondered if she had followed his orders.

***

Lydia had not really been surprised at Cade's anger, but he had never sent her to the corner before. She really didn't want to do it and thought about making a break for it. But where would she go? In the end, she figured it was best to do as he said. She had pulled down her jeans and panties and then realized that when she put her nose in the corner, her already stinging bottom was forced out into an embarrassing and vulnerable position. Nothing had prepared her for this deep humiliation. But maybe, if he found she had followed his orders, he wouldn't be so angry. She waited for maybe fifteen minutes, that seemed forever, before she heard his footsteps in the hall.

***

Cade saw that Lydia had left the door open, so as soon as he got to the doorway, he could see her standing just he had directed, with her nose in the corner and her bare bottom on display. He had to admit that seeing the pink imprint of his hand on that little bottom and hearing her quiet sniffling turned him on, but he was here to teach her a lesson.

She knew why she was here, so he did not begin with a lecture. Instead, he went directly to the corner, grabbed her upper arm and sat down on the bed, which for Lydia, was high off the ground. When he placed her over his knee, she couldn't reach the ground and had to grab his leg. Cade said nothing but just began spanking. Later in their relationship, she would come to expect a warmup beginning to some spankings, but today, Cade was too angry, and from the very first smack, Lydia was bawling. He spanked in the same spot three or four times, which really lit a fire, and then moved to another spot. When he had completely burned her bottom, he moved down to her thighs. That was much more painful and she was steadily screaming when she could catch a breath. Finally, after a long time, he stopped, and continuing to hold her over his knee with his hand on her flaming butt, he waited for her to calm a little. Then he tipped her up onto his lap, grabbed tissues to clean off her face, and held her while she cried it out.

Finally, Lydia whimpered, "I'm sorry, Cade. I'll never do that again."

"I'm glad to hear it, but your punishment is not over, baby."

"What?" Lydia wailed as she moved to protect her bottom with her hands. "Please, no more, Cade."

He moved to remove her jeans and panties from her ankles where they had ended up and stood her up. "You know I think naughty girls remember better when their bottom is bare, so you are going into the kitchen, sit your hot little butt in a chair, and write out what you did today that got you a spanking and how that spanking felt."

Cade had humiliated Lydia a few times now, but nothing

compared with this. She was about to rebel, but one look at his face made her think that was not a good idea at all.

"Go sit down. I'll bring you a pen and paper."

It hurt so much to sit with a freshly spanked bottom on that hard kitchen chair that Lydia could barely concentrate on her "assignment." When Cade pointed out that the sooner she began, the sooner she could stand up, she made herself get to work. It took her about thirty minutes to write it well enough to meet his approval, but he finally let her up.

"Go get into pajamas now. You've had a long day." When Lydia huffed, he said, "I will not stand for any sulking. Got it?"

"Yes, sir. I got it," Lydia said as compliantly as she could.

When she came out of the bedroom looking soft and sleepy, Cade invited her to sit on his lap.

"Your bottom still sore, baby?"

"You know it is, Cade. Stop teasing me."

"Okay, how about if I take your mind off your stinging butt?"

He began gently running his hand up and down her back, which was very relaxing. Then his hand moved down inside her pajama bottoms and his finger found her folds. She was as wet as he expected, so he inserted one finger and then moved to her clit.

"Ah! Cade! What are you doing?"

"I'm making it all better. Are you feeling all better?"

Now Lydia was breathless. "Oh yes, yes, yes!" she cried as she felt a crescendo of euphoria. In just a few moments, Lydia let out a scream of pleasure as she rode Cade's fingers until she was sated.

He was right. He had certainly taken her mind off of her punished bottom.

He picked her up, carried her to the bedroom, and with no protest, she nestled into the soft bedding. Cade chuckled as he observed the satisfied smile on her face as it melted into sleep.

## Chapter 20

Cade and Connor were very pleased with the work ethic and skill development of the hearing-impaired students and said so at a progress meeting at the high school in November. The apprentice program that employed Lydia to facilitate and integrate the students into the actual construction workforce was more successful than anyone had hoped. The students and their families were happy as were the school administrators who had pushed for the program. Interest from state legislators had also been garnered as Three Rivers High School was the largest high school in the vicinity of the state capital. The businesses that had supplied grant money were especially pleased with recent media coverage on local television stations, and there was even a statewide network news team coming to do a story on the program in the next week.

Lydia's friend, and now also Connor's girlfriend, had also been at the meeting as she was sometimes called in to help out as an ASL substitute when Lydia needed to be gone.

Cade, Connor, Lydia and Sarah all left the meeting feeling pretty pumped and decided to celebrate by going out to eat.

As they were still being as discreet as possible with their relationships, they decided to make a short trek to an out of town tavern known for great ribs. The four of them had never been together socially and it turned out to be so much fun. The McCauley brothers got along like good friends and Lydia and Sarah had met as colleagues and now were good friends. It seemed like the perfect end to a great day until near the end of the evening. Connor, who had gone up to pay the tab, came back and motioned to Cade to come with him. Lydia could see them talking quietly together and looking over at her.

They didn't say anything to the girls but when they came back a few minutes later, Cade looked very serious and said, "You know, I've got a lot going on tomorrow. If you're ready, Lydia, I'd like to go home."

Lydia sensed there was something wrong but agreed and got her things. They said their goodbyes and she noticed that Cade seemed to be looking for something in the parking lot. Once they got in the truck, she asked, "What's wrong, Cade? It seems like something happened when you went to talk to Connor."

"No. Everything's okay, baby. Nothing to worry about."

Lydia was not reassured, as she knew Cade well enough to know different. But she let it go.

That night, Lydia noticed that when they made love, Cade was a little more intense—one could even say urgent. And when he insisted she fall asleep wrapped in his arms, the spidey sense she had that something was wrong went on alert.

The next morning, Cade was showered and dressed before Lydia even woke. When she padded sleepily out to the kitchen, he said, "Oh, baby, I'm sorry I woke you. Go back to bed. It's early yet. I've got to run a few errands and pick up some supplies for the week."

"I might as well get up too. I can run to the grocery store

and get my car washed," she said as she grabbed a mug for coffee.

"No!" Cade said a little too loudly. "I don't want you going anywhere while I'm gone. Wait until this afternoon and we'll go together."

Now, Lydia was annoyed. "All right, Cade, I've had it! There is something you are not telling me. You have behaved strangely since Connor talked to you before we left last night. Tell me what happened. Please."

Cade looked her in the eye, paused, and then picked her up to deposit her on the counter.

"Oh, this must be serious. Counter talk is always serious." Lydia grinned.

"It *is* serious. And I want you to listen to me carefully."

"I'm listening, Cade," she said contritely.

"Last night, the bartender at the tavern was an old friend of Connor's. He told Connor that Daryl Caruthers and his brother had been sitting at the bar when we came in and started talking smack about Connor and me. Connor's friend kept close to the brothers so see what he could find out."

"Well, what did they say?" Lydia asked, her eyes wide.

"They made a lot of threats about what they wanted to do to Connor and me and, more specifically, what they wanted to do to you. The bartender heard them talking about a plan, but then they picked up their food to go and left. Connor ran out to the parking lot to see if he could stop them, but they were already gone."

Cade was pretty upset talking about it. He pounded a fist on the counter that made Lydia start, and then he began to pace in front of her. Lydia waited quietly.

"I think we have become complacent about the danger of having those idiots angry at us. It's been a few weeks now and I haven't kept as close an eye on you as I think I need to. We're going back to the plan where you let me know where you are at all times and check with me when you go somewhere—anywhere. Do you understand, Lydia?"

Lydia tried not to get upset, but the idea of being a prisoner in her own life made her miserable. "Cade, I don't want to live like that. If we are trapped by the threats of those jerks, haven't we let them win?" She broke down in tears. "How long do we have to live like this? Can't we do anything?"

Cade swept her up off the counter and took her to sit on his lap in his recliner. He placed her facing him on his lap and reached up to wipe her tears with his thumbs.

"Baby, don't cry. Connor and I have been thinking about this and we think we have a plan."

"What kind of a plan?"

"A plan that will get the Caruthers put away for a long time."

"That sounds dangerous! What are you going to do?"

"I'm not talking to you about it right now. But I can tell you that for it to work, you need to be as safe as I can make you, and that means always letting me know where you are or preferably sticking with me."

"But, Cade…" she fairly wailed. "I hate that idea! Besides being trapped, now I'm afraid for you and Connor."

Cade pulled her to him and kissed her face and eyes, then put her face into his neck. "Lydia, you don't need to be afraid. Everything will be okay. I'll take care of you. Do you believe me?"

"I believe you, Cade."

"Of course, you need to cooperate completely."

Lydia gave out a little moan.

"Do I need to remind you what will happen if you don't?"

Lydia said nothing.

"Lydia!" he said in a warning voice that she knew well by now.

"Yes, I understand, you Neanderthal. If I don't do what you say, you'll set my bottom on fire."

"Damn straight," he said and then moved in to give her the kind of kiss that made her forget everything but her love for him.

## Chapter 21

The next few days were difficult. Cade was on edge, and it seemed that he worried about Lydia even when she was just in another room. He preferred to go with her wherever she needed to go, rather than just let her check with him, so she often had to wait until he was available. Lydia's patience with the situation was running thin and his nerves about the Caruthers' threats were sometimes frayed. Once or twice, she thought she had pushed him too far and that she would end up over his knee, but so far she had escaped with a couple of bare bottomed reminder swats as he quickly bent her over the counter or back of the sectional. Sarah had complained that Connor was on edge too. Whatever "plan" the McCauley boys had conjured up to "handle" the Caruthers' threat, they were not talking about it, and so far nothing had happened.

So, by the time Thursday rolled around, Lydia was stir crazy and anxious to see her friend and talk. It was an in-service day at school so students were off and teachers were done early at 2:00. When Sarah suggested they go to the

Raveno for a late lunch, Lydia agreed immediately. She could get a couple hours of freedom and still be home before Cade.

Ordering a couple of light beers and sharing a big Raveno burger, the girls had a great time catching up. At one point, they were laughing so hard, they noticed some of the customers were looking at them. Lydia was having so much fun that she lost track of time and was halfway through her second beer when she realized it was already 5:30. She looked at her phone and said in a panic, "Oh, no! I have to get home before Cade—

"Calm down, Lydia, why do you have to be home first?" Sarah said, surprised.

Lydia explained the entire Caruthers' threat to her, stopping short of telling her how she knew Cade would react to her going out this afternoon without even checking in. Lydia's face turned pink and just when she thought she had worked up the courage to give Sarah details on just how awful Cade's spankings were, Sarah said, "Well, if he's anything like Connor, he'll be waiting at home to bust your ass."

Lydia's eyes nearly popped out of her head. Then she remembered that Sarah had been dating Connor ever since the week she had subbed for Lydia at the site. They had never really had time to talk about how that was going. She put down her coat and sat back down. She had to hear about this. "What do you mean 'anything like Connor'?'"

"You know, Connor is not as, well, domineering as Cade, but he still needs to be in charge. A couple of weeks ago, Connor stopped by my house without calling first. I was out on the deck smoking."

"I thought you quit," said Lydia.

"Yeah, well, I have mostly, but when I am anxious, I still reach for one. I keep some hidden in the fridge. I was listening to music, so I didn't hear or see Connor until his big body blocked my sun. To make an unfortunate story short, he took issue with me smoking. I mean, he made a really big deal of it. I got mad and began arguing. I got so mad that I let fly with some profanity."

"Oh no!" said Lydia, knowing what Cade would do in that case.

"Before I knew what was happening, Connor had grabbed my cigarette to snuff it out and then grabbed me. He put me over his shoulder and made his way inside to my bedroom. I was spluttering, kicking, and making a huge fuss until he let loose and walloped my bottom. I was shocked! But not as shocked as I was when he put me over his knee, pulled down my pants and panties and began spanking me. Oh my God, Lydia! I could not believe how much it hurt. And he wouldn't stop until I promised never to smoke again, which I did right quick. But then he kept spanking until I apologized for the language I used."

"What happened then?" asked Lydia breathlessly.

"He finally stopped and sat me on his lap and comforted me," Sarah explained. "And then I remembered what you said about feeling protected and cared for. I mean, it hurt like the devil and I was mad, but more than that, my heart nearly burst to think he cared that much for me. Isn't it ridiculous that there I was crying on his lap after a long, hard spanking and still thinking I was falling in love? Is that how you feel about Cade?"

"Oh, Sarah," she said. "Yes!"

Sarah stood and gave Lydia a hug as she sat on the barstool. "Aren't we a pair? Falling for two bossy brothers? And aren't we lucky to have each other to talk to?"

Lydia gave Sarah another hug but then said, "I don't think I'm going to feel so lucky when I get home. I know I'm in trouble. I've got to go—right now!"

"Are you going to tell Cade where we were?"

"Um, no. So please don't mention it to Connor."

Suddenly, Sarah looked stricken. "Oh, Lydia, I think I already told Connor I'd be meeting you here. I'm so sorry."

Lydia got a sinking feeling but said, "It's not your fault, Sarah, you didn't know. Maybe they won't talk about it. I'll try calling you later. Wish me luck!"

Lydia headed out to the back parking lot while Sarah made her way to the street in front where she was parked. She made her way down the long back hallway of The Raveno, past the kitchen and utility closets. It was almost 6:00 and had begun to get dark. Cade would be furious! She was nearly to the back door when it slammed open and in walked Daryl and David Caruthers. They blocked the hallway completely. Lydia recognized them immediately but kept moving.

"Excuse me please," she said as tried to hide her face behind her hair and push past them.

"Whoa! Hold on there, little lady! The night's just gettin' goin'. Come on in and have drink with us."

Lydia kept moving to push past them while she said, "No, thank you. I was just leaving."

Suddenly, Daryl grabbed Lydia's arm and held her chin so he could look at her face. "Well, look who we have here, brother! It's that little bitch that done lost us our jobs."

Now Lydia could smell the liquor on his breath but she said, "I don't know what you are talking about. I've never seen you before."

"Nice try, bitch, but I would recognize you anywhere. Since your "boyfriend" fired us for talking to that little deaf bitch, we haven't been able to find work. You ruined our lives! And I plan to make you pay." He must have anticipated that she would scream, so in a flash he was behind her with one of his big, dirty paws over her mouth.

"Come on, David, let's have a little fun with this one," he said with a sneer as his grip on her arm tightened painfully. With his hand still over her mouth, he dragged her through the back door. Lydia fought like a wildcat and tried biting the hand over her mouth but with no effect.

"Hell, get me some duct tape out of the truck, David."

His brother ran to a nearby truck, got some tape, tore off a piece and slapped it over Lydia's mouth. All hope of screaming or yelling out was gone. There were two of them and just one of her. They were big, angry and drunk, and she began to panic. But she couldn't give up. She swung her booted foot out to Daryl's shins and heard it connect and then heard a satisfying groan of pain.

"You little cunt! That hurt!" Daryl yelled just before he hauled off and backhanded her so hard that she fell to the ground. She saw stars and, for a moment, couldn't move.

Just as he grabbed her again and yanked her back up, she heard a loud, deep voice behind her say, "Let go of her or I'll kill you! Back off!"

It was Cade. She didn't know how he had gotten there, but she was so glad to hear his voice. Her eyes found his and she whimpered under the tape.

"I'm right here, baby, hold on," he said as he stalked closer to them.

"Goddammit! Start the truck, David!" Then he looked at Cade and said, "She's comin' with us!"

Cade kept moving toward them. Lydia hoped never again to see the fury she saw in his face at that moment. Daryl wrapped his arm around her neck from the back and began dragging her to the truck. She pulled at his arm and began to choke. Between choking and the duct tape over her mouth, she couldn't breathe. She had never been more frightened. She closed her eyes and felt she must be ready to faint. Suddenly, there was a knife at her neck!

"Don't move, bitch," he said to Lydia and then yelled to Cade, "Back off or I'll cut her!"

Lydia stopped struggling and let him drag her. Just then,

she heard a crack and a grunt and the arm around her neck fell away. She began to slide to the ground, but Cade had her in his arms before she fell. She turned to see Daryl slump to the ground, unconscious, while Conner stood there with a wrench. Connor then turned his attention to the brother in the truck, but before he could reach the truck, David had grabbed a gun, taken a shot at Cade and sped off.

Cade was unhurt and moved to pick up Lydia. "You're okay, baby. I've got you. Everything will be okay." Cade was speaking quietly to her as he carried her to his truck. He opened the door and sat her on the seat. "Can you sit by yourself?" he asked.

She thought he was leaving, so she grabbed at his shirt, frantic that he might go.

"No, babe. Look at me. Just sit up so I can check you over and get this tape off."

She looked into his eyes and immediately felt that she would be okay. He began to pull gently at the tape, but it wasn't coming off. She motioned for him to just rip it off.

"Are you sure, Lydia? It's going to sting."

She gave him a pleading look and he grabbed one end of the tape and yanked. In one motion, it was off. Lydia's hands flew to her mouth as Cade pulled her face to his chest and rocked her. "You'll be okay, baby. I've got you."

---

Cade was horrified at the swelling, bruises and cuts on the side of Lydia's face and his hands were moving gently all over her body, checking for any more damage. Connor approached his brother so see if he needed help. Connor had never seen Cade so shaken. His face was ashen and there were tears streaming down his face. He loved this girl and he thought he had lost her. Connor put his hand on his brother's shoulder and said,

"She's okay, Cade. This attack will land them both in jail. The cops said they have an APB out for David, and Daryl will be handcuffed to a hospital bed."

Just then Lydia heard sirens and Connor's voice say, "There's the police and hopefully an ambulance." Then he said, "Lydia, hang on, you're going to be okay."

Before she could answer, she heard Sarah's voice wail, "Oh, Lydia, you poor thing! Are you okay?"

"Goddammit, Sarah, didn't I tell you not to come out here? Do you ever listen?"

"Connor, please! I had to see if she was okay. I saw him haul off and hit her and then she fell to the ground. Will she be okay?" She ran to Lydia and said, "I'm so sorry. I shouldn't have left you alone. I'm so sorry." They were both crying hard now. Sarah looked up at Connor then and said, "Connor, I'm so sorry."

"I know you are. Come here." Connor put his arm around her and rocked comfortingly.

Lydia had calmed now and Cade was gently wiping her tears. The police arrived at the same time as the ambulance. The paramedic checked out Lydia and wanted her to go to the hospital to see if there was anything broken. Her face was bruised and bleeding where that animal had hit her. Cade lifted her into the ambulance and rode along, holding her hand to the ER.

Hours later, after Lydia had been checked out—no broken bones but some nasty bruises and a cut on her face—the doctor recommended ice on and off all night and prescribed some pain pills. Then the police took statements from Connor, Cade and Lydia.

Daryl Caruthers had been admitted to the hospital for head wounds. He had a police guard, as he was going to be charged with assault and attempted kidnapping. A roadblock had apprehended David Caruthers, who was now cooling his heels in jail, awaiting charges.

The hospital insisted that Lydia use a wheelchair to get to Cade's truck and when they got in the parking lot, Lydia suddenly realized she had never spoken to Connor. "Oh, Connor! Thank you so much for helping to save me tonight. I'm so sorry I was so much trouble. I was so stupid."

Connor hunched down in front of Lydia and took her hands. "I'm so glad we got there in time. Tonight, you just go home and let my brother take care of you."

"But I'm so sorry," wailed Lydia as she began to cry.

"I know, Lydia, but everything will be okay," Connor said sweetly as he rubbed his thumbs over the backs of her hands.

Then Sarah was in front of her. "Don't worry about anything, Lydia, I'll sub at the site for you tomorrow so you can rest and heal, and I'll call you after school." Then Sarah's hands began to move as she signed, "Don't worry about Cade. He can't spank you now. He loves you so much."

Lydia smiled at Sarah and signed, "We'll see. I hope you are right."

"All right, girls, enough secret language. It's time to go," said Connor as he put his arm around Sarah and pulled her away from Lydia.

Cade had been quiet but now gently lifted her into the truck and buckled her in. "Come on, baby, let's get you home and comfortable."

## Chapter 22

C ade didn't even want to let Lydia out of his sight long enough for her to take a shower, but she brushed him off. He helped her get into pajamas, got a couple more pain pills in her, and offered to make her a smoothie, as her jaw was stiff from the blow she took.

"Please, Cade, I really feel better. You've done all you can do and I love you for it. Can you just lie with me while I fall asleep?"

At that moment, he would do anything for his hurt little girl. Cade's emotions were all over the place. He had never been so frightened as when he saw Daryl Caruthers threatening Lydia with a knife to her neck. Feeling helpless was unfamiliar for him, as was the guilt he felt that he had not protected her. Then, too, he was furious at her for going out to a tavern without telling him. If she had obeyed him, Lydia would not be lying in his bed with bruises forming over one side of her face and traumatized by the Caruthers' attempt to hurt her. When she healed, she was in for a spanking she would not forget.

He watched her as she slept and decided that he would ask

her to marry him. He wanted to be with her, to love and protect her for the rest of her life. It didn't matter that they had not known each other that long, Cade knew she was the one. He barely slept as he lay with her wrapped in his arms, planning how and when to ask her to be his wife.

The next day, the bruising was full blown—swollen and purple. Lydia had a swollen lip and a black eye. Cade insisted she do nothing but sit with ice packs on her face all day.

Later in the day, the police stopped over to explain that they had both brothers in custody. They had been charged with attempted kidnapping and attempted murder. It turned out that they had both also been discovered to have a history of domestic abuse with former girlfriends, one of whom had been permanently disfigured. The detective thought they might get fifteen to twenty years, and they were not being released on bail.

Connor and Sarah brought pizza and smoothies late in the day and celebrated the fact that the Caruthuerses were out of the picture and Lydia was safe and getting better. The school system had offered Lydia a leave of absence until she felt ready to come back, but she didn't want to take it. Cade reminded Lydia that, at least for now, her face was pretty beat up and it would be best to wait until she was looking herself again. So, Sarah would take her place for the upcoming week, and then they'd go from there.

Lydia was sitting at the kitchen island while Cade cleaned up when, suddenly, he grabbed her and sat her on the counter. As this was where Cade always put her when he wanted to talk seriously, Lydia got worried. She knew that Cade had to be angry that she had put herself in so much danger. She had not followed his directions to let him know where she was and had gone to the bar without him. He hadn't said anything so far, but she knew he would address her disobedience at some point. Maybe that time was now.

"Oh, Cade, I am so tired. I don't want to talk about anything serious right now. Can it wait until tomorrow? Please?"

"No, little girl, it can't. And you will sit right there and listen to me. Do you understand?"

Lydia didn't like where this was going but she responded, "Yes, sir."

Cade took her hands in his and said, "Look at me, Lydia."

She did as she was told.

"The first time I saw you at the site, signing with a group of students, I knew you were special. My feelings for you became deep, and more serious, every time we were together. Some might say we have not been together long enough for me to know, but I do know. I love you, Lydia Lang."

It was such a sincere and loving speech that tears welled in Lydia's eyes. She tried to pull her hands away as she said, "Oh, Cade—"

He interrupted and held her hands in place. "No. Let me finish. I want to be with you for the rest of our lives. I want to marry you, Lydia."

She gasped as he reached into his back pocket and brought out an exquisitely styled diamond ring.

"Will you do me the honor of becoming my wife?"

Lydia squealed, threw her arms around his neck, and began to cry. "Oh, yes, yes, yes, yes, yes! I love you, Cade McCauley!"

He took her left hand and reverently put the ring on her finger. Then he leaned in for a deep and passionate kiss to seal the deal.

As he pulled away, Lydia looked down at the ring that meant so much and whispered, "I am so happy, Cade!"

"I'm glad you're happy because we also have some unpleasant business to take care of today," Cade said as he put his hands around her waist and held her there.

"What? What do you mean? Unpleasant? Today, when we just got engaged?" Lydia was shocked.

"I believe I need to begin as I plan to go on, and you knew you would be in trouble when you completely disobeyed me and went out without telling me. That is never going to happen again."

"But, Cade," she whined, "you can't spank me on our engagement day."

"This is just the right time for you to remember how I handle little girls who put themselves in danger. You will want to do exactly as I say, or things will go worse for you. Understand?"

Lydia wrung her hands and a tear slipped down her cheek, but she knew this would be part of her life with Cade. And she loved him. "I understand, Cade," she said softly.

"Go into the bedroom, put your nose in the corner, and bare your bottom. Wait for me."

As Lydia slowly walked to the bedroom, she realized that she knew this was how it would end when she had disobeyed him. And she knew that he meant to impress upon her how their life together would go on from here—forever.

# Hannah Kane

Hannah Kane dove right into writing with her first romance series, *Love Signs*. The first book, *Signs of Love* was released in August 2021 with others - *Signs of Courage* and *Signs of Hope* - following later in the year.

Hannah believes the gift of story came from her mother and was so deeply instilled that she became a children's librarian and professional storyteller.

Hannah now spends her days working part time in a crisis center, enjoying family and friends in the comfort of the lake-side neighborhood where she grew up, and of course, happily writing romance.

Don't miss these exciting titles by Hannah Kane and Blushing Books!

*Signs*
Signs of Love
Signs of Courage
Signs of Hope

## Blushing Books

Blushing Books is the oldest eBook publisher on the web. We've been running websites that publish steamy romance and erotica since 1999, and we have been selling eBooks since 2003. We have free and promotional offerings that change weekly, so please do visit us at http://www.blushingbooks.com/free.

## Blushing Books Newsletter

Please join the Blushing Books newsletter
to receive updates & special promotional offers.
You can also join by using your mobile phone:
Just text **BLUSHING** to 22828.

Every month, one new sign up via text messaging will receive
a $25.00 Amazon gift card, so sign up today!